Enforcer Delanrue Drudeson is a komodo dragon shifter who's known as the intense brother, the unapproachable one, but he has his reasons. Keeping his brothers safe from a sadistic alpha while growing up meant he'd had to be a careful, manipulative adult . . . from a very early age. Specializing in interrogation for the last several decades, Delanrue is happy with his life. Then he walks into a secure room where he's supposed to question the occupant by any means necessary — Midget Suvergy, a guinea pig shifter.

Except, one sniff tells Delanrue that Midget is his mate — the other half of his soul. Knowing the mate-pull could easily compromise his judgment, he immediately assigns the interrogation duties to another. That doesn't stop him from walking back into that room to be with him. Midget claims just to have been in the wrong place at the wrong time, and to Delanrue's relief, his words scent true.

Then word comes down that Midget is wanted for the murder of a member of his guinea pig muddle. Delanrue isn't stupid. It's easy to see that Midget is no killer, no matter what anyone says. Can Delanrue's connections keep Midget safe long enough to clear him from the conspiracy dogging his steps?

Interrogation Techniques
Copyright © 2020 Charlie Richards
ISBN: 978-1-4874-3168-6
Cover art by Angela Waters

Published by eXtasy Books Inc or
Devine Destinies, an imprint of eXtasy Books Inc

Look for us online at:
www.eXtasybooks.com or www.devinedestinies.com

# INTERROGATION TECHNIQUES
## SHIFTER'S REGIME BOOK SIX

BY

## CHARLIE RICHARDS

# DEDICATION

*When there are too many irons in the fire . . . stoke the fire and keep on burning.*

# CHAPTER ONE

"You're coming, Del, and that's the end of it!"

Enforcer Delanrue Drudeson turned his head just enough to arch his left eyebrow as he pinned a side-eyed look on his youngest brother — Dakota.

"Seven," his brother continued. "And if you want that shit microbrew stuff you like, you can bring it your own damn self."

Delanrue — Del to his brothers and *only* his brothers — growled softly under his breath. It wasn't because he didn't want to go to his youngest brother's Christmas party. Actually, Del did.

Instead, Del fought against curling his lip because he spotted Glade Kanston strutting down the corridor toward them. He found the other Shifter Council enforcer to be a piece of entitled, self-absorbed shit. Del had hoped he would be implicated in working with one of the rogue ex-councilmen, just so he could arrest him and never have to deal with him again.

Too bad that hadn't happened.

Glade was not only straight as an arrow with a stick up his ass, that stick meant he wasn't going to break any shifter laws, either.

*Guess that's a good thing.*

"I mean it," Dakota pressed, clearly misunderstanding his vocalization. He waved his finger under Del's nose while adding, "If you're not there by seven, I'll send — "

"I'll be there," Del stated in a low, gruff voice. "Stop your bitchin'."

1

Del couldn't care less who Dakota thought he could send to get him to comply. If he didn't want to go somewhere, he wouldn't. The only time he did something that he would rather not was when he was ordered to by the Shifter Council.

Seeing as Del loved his job as an enforcer and interrogator for the Shifter Council, that didn't happen too often.

"Good," Dakota replied, sounding smug. Then he must have spotted who actually held Del's attention, for he muttered, "Oh."

Del grunted but left it at that, since by then, Glade had drawn close enough to be within earshot. Trying to avoid true interaction, he met the lion shifter's gaze and dipped his chin in the barest of nods. Then Del focused his attention down the hall past the man.

From the corner of his eye, Del saw that Dakota did much the same thing. Then his brother returned to their conversation, and Del knew it was a ploy to keep Glade from attempting to engage them. Especially since Del knew Dakota was already aware of that which he spoke.

"Dane said he might be bringing a date," Dakota stated, a chuckle in his tone. "If he can convince the lady to join him, that is." With an open laugh, his brother added, "Guess our brother is having trouble convincing her that he's sincere."

"Probably because he's not," Del replied absently. Shaking his head, he thought about their middle brother's desire to date a human woman named Linda. "She's not his mate. I don't see why Dane's bothering. He can never reveal what we are to her, and he'll have to dump her eventually anyway."

Del had never understood why a shifter would date someone who was not only *not* a paranormal, but not their fated mate. There was no future there. Besides, even if they did decide to date a paranormal, Fate could place their mate in their path at any second.

Even though Del had warned his brothers of that very

thing on many occasions, both of them had been in and out of many relationships over the nearly two centuries they'd lived. Del would sit back and watch, and when their liaison inevitably fell apart, he'd helped his brothers mend their hearts.

"Dane is dating some poor hapless woman?" Glade smirked, stopping to stand in their path. He even crossed his arms over his chest as if that would make him some immovable object. "I bet he hasn't even let the lady know he's a dick licker. Maybe I should swing by tonight and let her know."

Del twisted his lips into a scowl as he glared at Glade. "Watch your mouth, Enforcer Glade," he ordered. As the council's lead interrogator, in the intricate hierarchy within those working for the Shifter Council, Del's position topped the lion shifter's. "Or someone on the council may hear about your slurs."

Glade tipped his chin up and attempted to look down his nose at Del and his brother. "I'm sure I wouldn't have anything to worry about. I work under Councilman Peregrine, after all," he stated, referring to an elk shifter who disagreed with homosexual matings. "He knows the true value of loyalty."

Councilman Georgio Peregrine's views had nearly caused him to lose his position, since he'd been backing other councilmen who were committing crimes against shifter-kind. When those crimes had come to light, the councilman had turned against them. That hadn't changed what he thought about gay matings, however. It just meant he was more subtle about where and when he voiced those views.

*Evidently, he shares them with Glade.*

Del knew better than to engage a bigot. Besides, he had places to be. He was in the middle of interrogating the last half dozen shifters who'd been captured when they'd taken down the now-deceased rogue ex-councilman Krakow.

*Good riddance.*

Taking a step to the left and forward, Del began rounding

the idiot standing in the middle of the hall. He noticed Dakota doing the same to his right. He peered beyond the man, turning his thoughts to the upcoming interrogation he needed to do.

That morning, Del had picked the brains of two bear shifters and one tiger shifter. Then he'd stopped to have lunch with Dakota. His afternoon would consist of the last three men they'd found.

Finally, the dungeons would be empty . . . of *those* people anyway.

Del knew a few shifters had been brought in for other crimes, but they hadn't been a priority. The council wanted all the information they could on Krakow's contacts, so they'd focused on his associates. Unfortunately, the wolf shifter hadn't shared too much about his organization with his minions — probably because he thought they were beneath him.

*I bet Pedro knows something, though.*

Pedro Kenbrook had been Krakow's accountant for over a hundred years. He'd created false accounting information to hide his boss's activities — payment for the sale of shifters as well as the money Krakow had paid to the mercenaries who captured them. Their cyber team had also uncovered files on the serums that the military was concocting by experimenting on shifters, although the formulas were incomplete.

*Can't wait to make that guy crack.*

They'd purposefully made Pedro wait until the end, allowing him to watch cell-mates disappear from around him.

"Hey, don't you walk away from me," Glade snapped, grabbing Del's upper arm. "I'm not done talking to you."

Del barely resisted rolling his eyes. With his thoughts on his duties, he'd nearly forgotten Glade was there. Pausing, he pinned the moronic lion with a cold gaze. "Not wise to put your hands on me," he stated, cutting a quick glance at where Glade had the audacity to touch him without permission.

Glade scoffed, although a hint of uncertainty crossed his

features, but only for a second.

*No sense of self-preservation.*

"Like I said," Glade claimed. "You can't do anything to me. I'm Peregrine's favorite."

Del was damn tempted to sock the other shifter anyway. He couldn't give a shit that Glade thought he was untouchable. Seeing Dakota move to stand next to him and taking in his brother's angry expression, he knew Dakota was on the same page and Glade was way out-classed.

*We'd wipe the floor with him.*

That was exactly why Del resisted.

Reaching over with his left hand, Del gripped the pinky and ring finger of Glade's hand. He wrenched them away from his bicep in what he knew was a painful hold. Hearing Glade hiss as his hand came away from him, Del released him, pushing his hand away further.

"We're done here," Del declared coldly, then began to turn away.

As if Glade had taken stupid pills that morning, he began reaching for Del's arm again. His expression had darkened to a thunderous look. Self-righteousness gleamed in his hazel eyes.

Del blocked Glade's attempt to grab him, and Dakota took it a step further. His brother snagged the lion shifter's outstretched wrist. Using his momentum, Dakota pushed Glade sideways, making him stumble several steps in the direction the shifter had been heading — toward the cafeteria.

"I'm gonna make you pay for that," Glade snapped, his hands fisting. He took a step back toward them. "When Councilman Peregrine hears how you pushed me around, you're gonna be sanctioned."

"If you keep grabbing me, the councilman will hear how we more than pushed you," Del warned. "I have places to be, and you're interfering with my duties."

Dakota scoffed, crossing his arms over his chest. A rakish

grin creased his features. "That means we're well within our right to extricate my brother from your grabby hands via any means necessary."

"Bullshit," Glade barked. "You were just eating lunch together. I know you, Delanrue." His eyes narrowed as if he had discovered some secret. "If you were in the middle of your duties, you wouldn't be having a long lunch with Dakota."

Although Del didn't care for the way Glade dropped his title of respect, he didn't comment on it. Instead, he replied calmly, "How I spend my lunch hour is not your concern, Enforcer Glade." Turning, Del began striding in the opposite direction. "Good day."

"I told you not to turn your back on me," Glade warned, anger filling his voice anew. "We're not done. I wanna know—"

"Enforcer Glade, stop hindering Enforcer Delanrue from returning to his duties," a deep voice ordered, drawing Del's attention to beyond the lion shifter. "I know you have somewhere you need to be, too."

Del spotted Mycroft Portent, an uber-dominant cheetah shifter, who worked as the head enforcer for the council. He ran a tight ship that Del appreciated. Mycroft had a frown creasing his lightly tanned features, and he was focused on Glade.

"Sorry, sir." Glade's tone immediately turned respectful. "I was just trying to get clarification on a matter."

"Get it another time," Mycroft ordered. Then he flicked his gaze between the brothers and gave them an almost infinitesimal nod. "I look forward to hearing what your afternoon's assignments have to say."

"Me, too," Del replied honestly as he returned the cheetah shifter's nod. "I'll have my report to everyone as soon as possible, Head Enforcer Mycroft."

"Good," the man replied.

Happy to get away from the annoying and obnoxious lion shifter, Del headed toward the interrogation wing. His brother broke off to the left, bidding him *good-bye* and *see you later*. Del responded by waving.

Del took the elevator down to the third underground level where the cells and interrogation rooms were located. As soon as he stepped off the elevator, a light, airy scent caught his attention. The pleasant fragrance was completely out of place within the hallway of cool concrete that ended in a heavy steel door which led to the cells.

To Del's increasing confusion, he felt the komodo dragon he shared his psyche with rumble with interest. His body warmed, and arousal began simmering sluggishly through his veins. He took in a slow, deep breath, hoping to squelch the unexpected and completely ill-timed rush of desire, but all that did was allow another surge of the pleasant aroma into his lungs.

*What the hell?*

Doing his best to dismiss the oddity, Del strode toward Germaine—a fellow enforcer and anaconda shifter. The tall, whipcord lean man stood outside the second interrogation room on the left. Two rooms were on each side of the hallway, just in case several had to be interviewed at once, so they could compare stories.

Of course, since a paranormal could normally tell when a person was lying, that didn't happen very often. Coincidentally, that was one of the things Krakow's serums had been trying to remedy. They'd done it, too, although the side effect meant the user had a distinct odor of patchouli. Now, every person smelling of that scent was suspect.

*In my opinion, anyway.*

"Hello, Enforcer Germaine," Del greeted the wiry black shifter. At six-foot-five, Del was nearly able to look the inch taller shifter in the eye. "Who's next on the list?"

"He says his name is Miggs. A guy we caught in his guinea

pig form at the warehouse. Claims he was just in the wrong place at the wrong time. He hasn't said anything beyond that," Germaine told him as he handed over a clipboard. When he sniffed, his black brows furrowed. "Uh, everything okay?"

While Del was known for being excellent at his job, he'd never become aroused by it. He figured the faint scent was confusing the snake shifter — or concerning him.

Grimacing, Del admitted, "There's a scent here that's getting to me." Then he focused on the page attached to the clipboard, trying to will away his burgeoning erection. "Don't worry about it. I'll still do —"

If Del had had a lightbulb in his brain, it would have suddenly flicked on.

Del grimaced as he peered toward the closed door. "Or maybe I won't," he muttered. "Hang on."

Cocking his head, Germaine didn't comment as Del reached past him.

Opening the door, Del didn't even need to take one step into the room. The light, airy scent pervaded the space with its deliciousness. His dragon rumbled with delight, urging Del to find the source and capture it for all time.

*Mine!*

Pinning his gaze on the shifter chained to the table, Del barely resisted the urge to run to him and free him from his bonds. The small man sat hunched at the table. His short hair hung lank against his skull, as if even the locks were admitting defeat.

Del wanted to wrap the little shifter in his arms and comfort him. He wanted to assure him that everything would be okay, and he would keep him safe. Then Del wanted to strip the baggy clothes to discover the body within.

Except, he had a job to do.

When the man — Miggs — lifted his gaze and peered at him

with fear-filled brown eyes from beneath his lashes, Del realized he couldn't.

Stepping backward, Del closed the door, and even putting that scant bit of distance between them tested his control.

*Shit! These mating urges are intense.*

"Call Enforcer Malone," Del murmured, tearing his gaze away from the closed door. He met Germaine's questioning look and told him, "That shifter, Miggs, is my mate. There's no way I can interrogate him objectively."

Germaine's jaw sagged open, and his eyes opened wide. Then his lips curved into a wide smile. "Damn, man. Congrats." Just as quickly, Germaine cast a worried look toward the room. "Hope he was telling the truth."

Del nodded. "Me, too."

Clamping his hand on Del's shoulder, Germaine offered him an encouraging smile. "We'll get it sorted." He took the clipboard, then used it to indicate the interrogation room. "Go comfort your mate. The little fellow looks like he could use it."

Nodding again, Del silently agreed.

As Del heard Germaine talking on his phone, he reopened the door and slowly headed inside, ready to meet the shifter who was about to turn his world upside-down.

*Still, I can't wait.*

An emotion flooded Del, and it took him a second to identify it.

*Joy.*

# CHAPTER TWO

*I'm cursed. That's the only explanation.*

Midget Suvergy—Miggs to his friends—*Oh, wait. I don't have any of those*—stared forlornly at the door where the sexy scary man had disappeared.

His guinea pig whined in his mind, and Miggs's heart ached in total agreement.

Par for the course for his life these last five years, the hits just kept on coming.

Miggs's own father—their guinea pig muddle's beta—had helped their alpha hold him captive, using him practically as a slave, as soon as he'd found out Miggs was interested in men. As he'd been part of an ultra-conservative muddle, he'd done his best to keep that nugget a secret for decades. One wrong smile at a waiter followed by the human writing his phone number on the receipt had caused the house of cards that Miggs called his life to come tumbling down.

Then the few guys Miggs had been hanging out with—men he'd called friends—had turned on him. Well, all but one had—Kenny. Unfortunately, Kenny hadn't been able to help much out in the open.

Still, Miggs appreciated the fact that Kenny was the reason he'd managed to get away.

After five years of never being able to leave the alpha's house, where he'd spent his days cleaning and helping the cook, Miggs had managed to escape. Kenny had slipped him money that he'd saved, a satchel of food, and a change of clothes. The man had even burned a cake, which had surely earned him a punishment, in order to leave the kitchen door propped open to air it out.

Miggs had been able to escape.

*I hope Kenny is okay.*

Of course, that thought brought Miggs back to his own predicament.

First, he'd been held captive by his own muddle because they thought a gay guinea pig had little use except as a slave. When he'd managed to escape, he'd hidden in what looked like a deserted warehouse. Except, it hadn't been.

Miggs had discovered too late that a group of rogue shifters were using the place as a base. He'd stayed in guinea pig form and hidden in the walls near the garbage bins in order to hide his scent. Before he'd been able to escape, another group of shifters had attacked.

The impressively savvy nose of a hyena shifter had discovered Miggs's hiding place, and he'd been taken captive, only to be tossed in the cells by the Shifter Council itself. Due to that, he'd hidden his true name. If his father or alpha learned of where he was through their connections, Miggs knew he would be dragged back to his muddle and beaten . . . before being made a slave again.

To top off his sucky life, his mate had taken half a step into the room, taken one look at him, and left again.

*He's probably telling the guard who brought me to the room to kill me.*

*Hell, both our lives would be better for it.*

As that uncharitable thought flitted through his mind, the door opened again.

Miggs snapped his gaze from where he'd allowed it to fall to the table. As he took in the huge, broad-shouldered man standing there, he couldn't stop his lips from parting. His heartrate spiked as he sucked in a sharp breath.

Once again, the spicy, earthy, masculine flavor of his mate teased his senses. His body responded instantly, just as the whispered comments of older members of his muddle had declared would happen should a shifter meet their fated mate. The hairs on his arms stood on end, and he felt his blood flood south, causing his prick to thicken.

Seeing the stranger's nostrils flare and the man's hazel eyes narrow, Miggs felt a niggle of embarrassment. They were in an interrogation room in the Shifter Council headquarters, he was a prisoner, and he was getting turned on. Except, he couldn't seem to control himself.

To Miggs's shock, the corners of the stranger's thick lips twitched. His expression turned intense as he swept his gaze over him. A long, pregnant pause hung between them, allowing Miggs to look his fill.

The stranger had to stand at least six-foot-four or more. His dark-blond hair had been pulled away from his face to be secured somehow behind him, showcasing his angular features and high cheekbones. He stared at him with a penetrating, hazel-eyed gaze that sent a shiver up Miggs's spine.

"Hmmm," the man began on a hum, a definite curve to his lips then. "I believe some introductions are in order." He slowly began stalking around the table, never taking his sizzling focus away from Miggs. "My name is Enforcer Delanrue Drudeson, the Chief Interrogator for the Shifter Council."

It took Miggs a second to register what the other shifter — Delanrue — was telling him. When it did, he gasped. "Ch-Chief In-Interrogator?"

"Indeed," Delanrue replied, his deep rumbling voice teasing at Miggs's senses. "And you are my mate. Miggs, is it?"

Miggs was too busy gaping to reply, watching the gorgeous, broad-shouldered specimen of maleness round the table and draw near to him. When Delanrue reached for him, Miggs finally yanked himself out of his lust-induced stupor. He flinched, leaning away from the big shifter.

"Easy, little mate," Delanrue all but purred even as he continued reaching for him. "You're my mate. I won't hurt you."

Then Miggs found himself lifted into the air. The chains connecting him to the table and floor clinked as he whimpered instinctively. As Delanrue lifted him into his arms, Miggs curled in on himself, uncertainty filling him.

"What are you doing?" he squeaked.

"Getting comfortable," came Delanrue's surprising response.

Before Miggs could even question what that meant, Delanrue settled in the chair he'd been in. Then he placed Miggs on his lap. Their sizes were on clear display by the move, with Miggs's ass easily cradled on Delanrue's huge thighs.

Delanrue slid down the chair a little, then relaxed against the back. Tightening his right arm around Miggs's waist, he tucked him close. With his other hand, Delanrue began rubbing up and down his opposite upper arm, soothing him while giving him something to lean against—his strong arm and torso.

Miggs's mind whirled. Sitting still on the big male's lap, he struggled to keep his breathing even. Each breath made it tougher than the last, since it drew more of Delanrue's earthy aroma into his lungs. That, in turn, caused his body to continue to heat with rising need.

When Miggs felt Delanrue dip his head and nuzzle his nose against his temple, it felt as if butterflies bumped in his belly.

"I do love the way you smell, too, my little mate," Delanrue purred into his ear. "And as much as I'd like to disconnect the corner camera, lay you out on this table, and lick every inch of your body as if you were my own personal feast, I think we have a few things to straighten out first. Don't you?"

Miggs's body flushed hot, then cold, as he processed Delanrue's words. After he'd heard the first part, his dick had swelled even more, pushing almost painfully against his borrowed sweats, since he'd been in guinea pig form when he'd been caught. Then Miggs realized Delanrue expected answers . . . he was an interrogator, after all.

"I-Is this some new bizarre interrogation technique?" Miggs blurted out his question. "Holding him and coaxing what you want to know from him?"

As Miggs spoke, a burn of jealousy tightened his gut.

To Miggs's surprise, Delanrue chuckled deeply into his ear. "No, my mate," he told him.

Sliding the hand up Miggs's arm, he gripped his nape. Delanrue used the firm but gentle hold to urge Miggs to meet his gaze. His intense hazel eyes peered down at him as if searching for every secret Miggs possessed.

"You are my mate, Miggs," Delanrue stated bluntly, verbally claiming him once again. "Your safety and happiness are my responsibility. Right now" — he released Miggs's neck and waved his hand around the room negligently — "this is not safe. I need to know what's going on so I can help fix it."

When Miggs just opened and closed his mouth, then open again, too shocked to find words, Delanrue touched his chin and urged it shut. All the while, a slightly crooked smile curved his lips. The expression would have appeared condescending, except for the appreciative gleam darkening the shifter's hazel eyes almost to green.

"So tempting to capture that mouth," Delanrue crooned. Then he shook his head sharply, and the lust cleared from his features. "First, we'll begin with something simple. I told you my name. Will you tell me yours? Is Miggs a nickname?"

When Miggs still hesitated, Delanrue skimmed his fingertips through his hair. The gentle massage to his scalp sent soothing tingles down his neck. He felt himself relaxing despite the tenuous situation.

"My hair must be really greasy," Miggs mumbled, leaning

more of his weight against Delanrue's broad chest.

"Hmmm," Delanrue hummed, not agreeing or disagreeing. "When we're done here, I'll take you to my quarters. The place has a massive shower, if you'd care to use it."

"Thank you," Miggs replied automatically, anticipation filling him. He hadn't had a decent shower since fleeing his muddle, and even before that, the shower he'd been allowed to use in the alpha's house was old, small, and the water pressure had sucked. Staring into Delanrue's serene expression, Miggs stated, "I guess if I can't be honest with my mate, I'm really in trouble."

Delanrue shrugged one broad shoulder—shoulders that looked like they could carry the weight of the world.

*I hope they can.*

"We don't know each other, yet," Delanrue pointed out. "But we will, in time. Time I'd like to have together." Curving a corner of his lips into a wry smile, he added, "You'll hear stories about what a bastard and asshole I am, and I won't refute them. I've done a lot of questionable shit in the name of obeying the Shifter Council and keeping our species safe."

Instead of worrying Miggs, hearing that reassured him. Forcing a tremulous smile, he whispered, "A badass may be exactly what I need to get out of this mess."

With a wink, Delanrue drawled, "Well, I did hear somewhere about a theory that Fate brings mates together when they need each other most."

Miggs smiled, liking that idea. Still—"I can't imagine you ever needing anyone."

"Maybe I need a sexy partner to care for so I don't slip even further into assholedom."

Snickering, Miggs shook his head. "I don't think that's a word."

"Meh," Delanrue replied dismissively. "So. Now we're back to helping each other." He arched one brow in question. "Miggs?"

Miggs knew he didn't truly have a choice. If it wasn't his mate asking nicely, someone else would demand the information. That person probably wouldn't ask so nicely.

"Miggs is a nickname," he admitted. "My birth name is Midget Suvergy, and I ran away from a muddle run by Alpha Shaun Rudger."

Delanrue hummed. "Midget, huh?" His grin turned teasing as he swept his gaze over Miggs, and he jiggled him just a bit in his arms. "You're small, but not that small."

Rolling his eyes, Miggs frowned at the big man. "Ha, ha."

With another wink, Delanrue told him, "Couldn't resist. Hopefully, you'll get used to my occasional bouts of inappropriate humor."

Miggs snickered softly. "Okay."

"So, you left your muddle. Weird word. Is that what a group of guinea pigs is called?"

"Some people use herd, too, but ours called it a muddle," Miggs told him.

Delanrue nodded as he asked, "Why'd you leave? How long ago was this?"

Having hidden his sexuality for so long, Miggs couldn't help but hesitate. Then he realized how foolish that was. After all, he was sitting on the lap of a man who happened to be his Fate-given mate.

*Gods, how did I get so lucky?*

"So, um, it's probably a familiar story, but Alpha Shaun leads an ultra-conservative muddle, so I hid my desire for men for decades." Miggs lowered his gaze to his hands where he twisted them together on his lap. "When a waiter hit on me and left me his phone number on my ticket, I couldn't help but blush." Miggs once again felt heat rise on his cheeks, telling him he was doing the same right then. "I-I was flattered because the guy was hot."

When Delanrue growled, Miggs snapped his attention to the big shifter's face. Surprise filled him, and he gasped. He took in the deep scowl marring Delanrue's expression and un-certainty caused tension to surge through him.

"Um, I-I —" Miggs stuttered.

Delanrue let out a deep sigh between pursed lips. "Sorry," he grumbled. His voice sounding gruff, he explained, "Hear-ing you talk about other hot guys is . . . annoying."

Realization filled Miggs, and he smiled shyly at his mate. "You're way hotter."

"Good." After the one word, Delanrue fell silent again.

Miggs picked up where he'd left off. "Um, anyway, be-cause I didn't insult the guy or say something rude about the phone number, um, and the blush," he added, thinking back to those few awkward moments while leaving the restaurant. "When I got home, one of the guys I'd been eating lunch with followed me, and he told my father about it." Seeing Delanrue's questioning look, Miggs explained, "My father is the muddle beta." Grimacing, he finished, "When he asked point-blank if I was attracted to that guy, I couldn't exactly lie. Ya know?"

Delanrue nodded. "So then what happened?"

Rubbing the back of his neck, Miggs continued, "That was about . . . five years ago, now." Then he explained about being a slave in the alpha's house and how, eventually, Kenny had helped him escape. "I had only been away from there for six days when I found the warehouse. I thought it was aban-doned." Miggs shook his head while hunching his shoulders. "When a whole bunch of shifters showed up, I was already inside. I shifted and hid in the walls, waiting for a chance to escape, but it didn't come before —" Waving his hand, Miggs didn't bother finishing.

Delanrue did it for him. "Before our teams came and cap-tured the rogues and you with them."

Miggs nodded.

Feeling Delanrue's cool, lightly calloused palm slide under

his chin, Miggs lifted his gaze to his mate's calm gaze.

"You know you're safe now, Miggs," Delanrue told him. "Right? This will be easy to clear up."

The thud of the door opening sounded through the room before Miggs could reply. A muscular, wiry redhead strode into the room followed by the guard that had escorted Miggs from his cell to the room. Another man joined them — a thickly built, dark-haired shifter.

"I'm afraid it's not going to be quite that easy to clear up," the redhead stated, his lips pinching in a tight line. Pointing to the camera, he explained, "We've been watching and listening."

Delanrue didn't seem surprised, saying, "I figured you would be." His eyes narrowed. "What do you mean it won't be easy to clear up, Enforcer Mycroft? Miggs really was in the wrong place at the wrong time. The rogue charges will be dropped, and I'll take him to my room to freshen up and relax while I question Pedro."

Miggs didn't know who that was, but he heard the way Delanrue growled the guy's name. His mate didn't like him.

The redhead, Mycroft, crossed his arms over his chest as he leaned against a wall. "As soon as Miggs told us his real name, Link ran it." His eyes narrowed as he pinned his gaze on Miggs. "Alpha Shaun reported that you went rogue and murdered Kenny when you fled."

Gasping, Miggs felt the blood drain from his face. "Kenny is dead? No!"

A cry of sorrow erupted from his throat as a shudder went through him.

# CHAPTER THREE

Del rubbed his hand up and down Miggs's back and did his best to squelch his angry snarl. His rage wouldn't help his clearly distraught mate. However, Del didn't temper the glare he pinned on Mycroft.

"You know that's bullshit," Del stated, pleased that his voice only held a hint of gruffness. He lifted a hand for an instant to indicate his quietly crying mate before returning it to rubbing his back. "This is not the response of a man who killed someone."

Hell, Del would know. He'd slain more than his fair share of shifters, humans, and other paranormals.

Mycroft unwound his arms and lifted his hands in placation. "I know. I heard the gratefulness in Miggs's voice when he spoke of Kenny helping him." Pushing away from the wall, the cheetah shifter added, "I'm only telling you why we can't just clear Miggs of being rogue." Before Del could answer, Mycroft smiled. "And congratulations, by the way. We'll get this sorted."

Del's anger at Mycroft evaporated. He should have known he had people who would help him. While his brothers would always be there for him, Del sometimes forgot that some of these shifters considered him a friend.

*Hell, Germaine asked me to help him move just last month. That's what friends do.*

"So, we need to find out what really happened to Kenny, then," Enforcer Malone stated from where he rested in the doorframe. The alligator shifter jutted his chin toward Miggs, a small smile curving his thin lips. "Hell, it's obvious Miggs didn't hurt him. That means someone else did."

"If he's even dead," Germaine cut in, cocking his head. "Maybe that was a lie just to have us out looking for Miggs."

Mycroft growled softly. "If that's the case, how many others have used the same ploy?" Curling his lip, he added, "The word of alphas in good standing aren't normally verified with an independent investigation."

"Time for another policy change," Malone commented drolly.

Germaine scoffed. "Oh, yeah. The council is going to *love* that suggestion. Ever since creating the investigative branch, we've been stretched thin as it is. Adding duties to them means we'll need even more of them."

"Yeah, but look how the changes are affecting us." Malone waggled his finger in Del and Miggs's direction. "Councilmen and enforcers are starting to find their mates. I hope it continues." His expression turned wistful. "I wanna find my mate."

Del had truthfully never given finding his mate much thought, but as he looked down at Miggs, he knew he would do anything for the man in his arms. Taking care of his cute shifter would definitely be a change, but he figured it would be a good one. Fate didn't make mistakes, after all.

Cradling Miggs's jaw, Del urged him to lift his chin and meet his gaze. The tears filling his mate's gorgeous brown eyes sent a spike of need through him—a need to fix the problem. Del just wasn't certain he could, but he was sure going to try.

"We're going to get to the bottom of this," Del assured his mate. "We know you didn't hurt your friend. That means someone else did."

"Could it have been Alpha Shaun or someone in the inner circle acting under his orders?" Mycroft asked. "Have they used that kind of punishment before?"

"That's not a punishment," Miggs snapped, turning to scowl at Mycroft. "That's a death sentence, and all he did was help free me."

Del couldn't help but smile at the bit of fire Miggs displayed. His mate's spunk caused Del's blood to heat. He wanted to find out if he would display such passion in other areas of his life . . . like with their bedplay.

Having always had a healthy appetite for sex, Del couldn't wait to explore everything with his sexy little shifter.

Mycroft rubbed a hand through his hair as he nodded. "If we discover he ordered Kenny's death, he'll be brought in, alpha or not. So will whoever carried it out."

"If he's even dead," Malone reiterated. "Maybe he's being locked up like you were, so no one knows he's actually alive."

"If he's even dead," Mycroft repeated, nodding. He began moving toward the door. "I'll put Investigator Ryzer on it right away." Then Mycroft pointed at them. "In the meantime, lay low. You're off duty until this is cleared up, Enforcer Delanrue."

Del shook his head, countering Mycroft. "What about Pedro?" He scowled. "I really want a go at him."

"Malone is here now," Mycroft stated, pointing at the shifter. "He can handle it."

"And if I run into any problems, I know where you are to get help," Malone told him even as a wicked grin curved his lips. He cracked his knuckles as a low chuckle escaped him. "But we both know I won't need it."

Groaning, Del rolled his eyes. He did know. Malone was almost as good at the job as himself.

"Just really wanted the chance to scare the shit out of that lying asshole," Del grumbled.

While Malone and Germaine laughed, Mycroft snorted and headed out of the room.

Del met Miggs's gaze and saw the surprise in his eyes. Lifting one shoulder in a half-shrug, he offered an unrepentant smile. "Warned you, didn't I?"

"Yeah," Miggs murmured with wide eyes. Then he blinked, and a shy smile curved his lips. "I'm okay with it."

"Good." Del dipped his head, his focus on Miggs's oh-so-tempting lips. When Miggs turned his head, stopping the action, Del frowned as something stabbed through his chest that it took a second to identify — the feeling of rejection. "Miggs?"

Miggs's cheeks took on a pinkish hue as he mumbled, "I-I, um, I haven't brushed in, well, a couple of weeks." Peering at him through his lashes, he admitted, "I don't like how my mouth tastes right now. How could you?"

Relief filled Del, and he nodded. "Then I look forward to getting you to my rooms so you can change that."

"And to help with that." Germaine stepped forward, holding up a keyring. "Let's get you out of here."

In a grand gesture that drew a snicker from Miggs — which, to Del's surprise, he liked the sound of — Germaine bowed low and unlocked his mate before indicating the open doorway.

Del wasted no time rising to his feet and carrying his still giggling shifter from the interrogation wing. As soon as he reached the door to his suite, he heard the rumble of Miggs's stomach. He pushed the door closed behind them and locked it, then lowered his mate to his feet.

Keeping Miggs close, Del rested one hand on his hip and used the other to cradle his jaw. "I would very much like the opportunity to wash you in the shower, but hearing your stomach, I feel the need to feed you, too."

His instincts to care for his mate were conflicting, and he struggled with which direction to choose. Then he remembered the advice he'd overheard a mated shifter give to Dakota on relationships

*Just because you're mates doesn't mean your relationship will be*

*all roses and sunshine. It still takes work. Always remember to communicate, and never go to bed angry.*

With those thoughts in mind, Del asked, "What would you like, Miggs?" He rubbed his thumb along his jawline as he eyed the lips he really wanted to taste. Noticing Miggs's hesitation, Del offered, "If you don't want me to wash you, I can fix you food. My kitchen isn't extremely well-stocked, but I can whip up omelets and potatoes, bacon and sausage. Or if you'd prefer a steak, I can zip to the cafeteria and order something from there."

As if anticipating his offerings, Miggs's stomach rumbled again.

"When was the last time you ate, my mate?" Del asked softly. He knew the prisoners were fed, but that didn't necessarily mean his mate had eaten much of it.

Miggs's brows furrowed, telling Del he had to think way too hard about it. "Um, yesterday my cellmate let me have a piece of bread," he murmured, sounding uncomfortable. "He was taken this morning after breakfast, and dinner hadn't been served, yet."

Del growled, making a mental note to find out who Miggs had been in a cell with. He was going to make certain abuse of a weaker shifter would be added to his crimes—assuming he was still alive. The stronger were supposed to care for those less powerful, not the other way around.

*How did we end up with so many asshole alphas that just don't understand that?*

Without bothering to voice that question, Del waited . . . and waited. His poor mate looked completely indecisive—his mouth opening and closing and his gaze shifting left and right. He wondered if the sweet man had ever been given the opportunity to make decisions for himself.

Then Del remembered that Miggs said he'd essentially been a slave for the last several years.

*He probably just doesn't remember how or doesn't feel confident enough.*

"How about this?" Del crooned softly, hoping to soothe his clearly uncertain shifter. "I'm going to take you into the bathroom and undress you. I'll start the shower, and you can take your time scrubbing down and getting clean. I'll leave a bathrobe hanging on a hook, and you can use it when you're done toweling off the water." He wasn't certain the straightforward instructions were the right approach—his mate was a grown man after all—but after everything that had happened, Miggs seemed a little overwhelmed. "After that, come out and sit at the dining room table. I'll have a late lunch ready for you."

As Del finished laying out his plans, he released Miggs's chin. He used the hold he still had on his waist to turn the much smaller male. Guiding Miggs through his front room, he enjoyed the way his mate fit against his side. The man couldn't have been more than five-foot-one and a buck-twenty soaking wet. From the feel of his hip through the sweats, Del knew Miggs was underweight.

*I can't wait to feed him up and help him reclaim himself.*

Del had seen flashes of what he was coming to think of as Miggs's true personality, and he looked forward to seeing him flourish.

"Here you go," Del said as he encouraged Miggs into the room. "There's shampoo, soap, and such in the shower stall. Help yourself to anything." While Del was loath to release his mate, he did it so he could reach past him, open the massive walk-in shower, and turn on the heads. Pointing, Del told him, "I'm going to leave it on the temperature I enjoy, so just adjust it to whatever you'd like. Okay?"

Turning back to meet Miggs's gaze, Del fought back a smile as he took in the way the small shifter peered around the nicely appointed space. For those who spent a fair bit of their time at Shifter Headquarters, the accommodations were excellent. Like all the enforcers, Del's place had a living room, a small kitchenette and dining space, a large bathroom, and a bedroom. The bathroom had two doors so that it could be accessed from both the living room and bedroom.

Del touched Miggs's shoulder, catching his attention. "Lift your arms, little mate," he encouraged. With a wink, he added, "Time to get you all wet."

Even as Del enjoyed the way Miggs blushed, he hid the look for a few seconds while tugging the overly large sweatshirt from his mate's body. He tossed it toward his laundry basket. Then he crouched before Miggs and gripped the waist of his sweatpants. Pausing, Del peered up at Miggs, silently asking permission.

Even though Miggs nibbled his bottom lip, he still nodded. *A win. I got him to make a decision.*

"Lift your legs, one at a time," Del ordered as he tugged the sweats down each one.

As Miggs obeyed and he removed the too-big pants, Del did his best to ignore the beautiful, semi-hard penis before his face. The scent of his mate was driving him crazy, but he controlled himself. He needed to see to *all* his mate's needs . . . not just the sexual ones. Fortunately, the way Del could clearly make out Miggs's ribs helped him keep in check.

*I need to feed my poor mate.*

Once Del had the sweats off, he rose and gripped Miggs's shoulders lightly. He used the hold to turn him. Unable to control himself completely, Del slid his palm down his mate's back and squeezed one small round ass cheek just a little as he pushed him forward with his other hand.

Miggs gasped and hopped forward a step. He peered over his shoulder at him with a wide-eyed gaze. His nostrils flared, and he clenched and released his hands. Even Miggs's eyes began to dilate while the scent of arousal flooded the bathroom.

"Get in the shower, my mate," Del ordered, his voice rough with his own rising need. He took a step backward, needing to put more space between them to keep from grabbing Miggs and saying, *to hell with it.* "I'll start some food." As his mate nodded and eased into the shower, Del asked, "Are you allergic to anything? Or is there anything you don't like?"

Del didn't want to accidently make something that Miggs hated.

"Um, I-I don't like . . . strawberries."

While Miggs's answer surprised him, Del nodded anyway. "Okay." With a wink, he turned and headed out of the bathroom calling, "No strawberries for you."

Just as Del closed the door, he heard, "Thank you."

"You're welcome," Del stated through the door.

Del strode swiftly to his small kitchenette and began pulling out supplies. As he started frying the pound of bacon along with another pound of sausage links, he pulled his phone from his belt. With a couple of swipes of his fingers, Del called Dakota.

Just as Del pulled the carton of eggs from the refrigerator, he heard Dakota pick up. In lieu of a greeting, Dakota stated, "I don't care what the excuse is. You said you were coming, so you better damn well be coming."

"I found my mate." Del laid it out there.

For several long seconds, no noise came through the line.

Del waited.

Finally, Dakota stuttered, "D-Did you just — did you just s-say what I-I think you said?"

Smiling, Del couldn't remember the last time he'd shocked the shit out of his brother. "Yes," he confirmed. "I found my mate."

Dakota's whooping cry boomed in Del's ear, making him grin.

It took a good two minutes before Dakota's exuberant cries died down, but Del didn't mind waiting some more. He loved that his brother expressed such joy on his behalf. If the situations were reversed, Del hoped he would have felt the same.

"Well, bring her on over with you," Dakota finally ordered, his grin coming through loud and clear. "Or him. Shifter? Human? Who is it? Where the hell did you meet? I just left you heading . . . to . . . the interrogation wing." Dakota's words slowed, and Del could just guess that his smart brother was putting the pieces together. "Del? Who is it?"

"Miggs was in the wrong place at the wrong time," Del told him. "And I'm going to bring him over tonight, because I think I'm gonna need you and Dane's help to keep him safe."

As much as it galled him, Del never second-guessed his gut, and his gut screamed of danger to his sweet little mate.

"Absolutely," Dakota responded without a second of hesitation. "Anything you need."

Del smiled.

He'd always been able to rely on his brothers.

As Del continued cooking, he told Dakota what little he knew.

# Chapter Four

"He must think I'm an idiot," Miggs muttered as he stood under the spray. "Couldn't even make a simple decision."

Even though the feel of the hot water cascading over his body felt beyond exquisite, Miggs's chaotic thoughts made it difficult to enjoy. He hadn't experienced such wonderful water pressure since . . . before. Before he'd blushed at the wrong comment. Before his father had demanded answers. Before he'd been enslaved by his own muddle.

Just *before*.

Sighing, Miggs forced his thoughts to the present. He couldn't change the past. Instead, he needed to look to the future.

*If my muddle has their way, I won't have one.*

"Can Delanrue really stop Alpha Shaun?" Miggs wondered out loud as he reached for the soap. Scrubbing over his body, he dared to hope. "Del." With a sigh, Miggs whispered his mate's name. "Fate brought me my mate, and he's a badass."

That thought drew a smile to Miggs's lips. Closing his eyes, he rubbed his soapy hands over his chest. For a few seconds, he imagined he'd agreed and invited Delanrue into the shower with him. He could have felt his mate's hands rubbing all over him, washing him, soothing his tired limbs.

The direction of his imaginings had a predictable reaction on his body. His blood flowed to his dick, and he began to harden. Having been at half-mast just from Delanrue's wonderful masculine scent, despite the stress of the situation, Miggs ended up rock-hard in no time.

Groaning softly, Miggs stared at his erection. He reached for himself, then paused. Nibbling his bottom lip, he peered through the glass toward the door.

Delanrue would undoubtedly be able to smell his release the second he left the bathroom.

*And I'd much rather have him touching me than doing it myself.*

With that thought in mind, Miggs hurried through the rest of his wash. He didn't know if Delanrue even wanted to bond right away, but he wanted to be prepared. With that in mind, he scrubbed at his skin, cleaning *everywhere*.

Once Miggs felt squeaky clean, he turned off the water and grabbed a towel. He rubbed himself dry as he peered around the bathroom. Spotting the robe hanging on the back of the door, he smiled.

Miggs didn't know when Delanrue had slipped into the room to hang it there, but he appreciated it none-the-less. Shivering in the steamy air—his body devoid of enough fat to keep him comfortable even in the warm space—he pulled on the robe. He tucked the too-large garment around himself and stood for a moment, enjoying the plush, soft fabric.

Pressing his nose against the collar, Miggs inhaled deeply. He nearly moaned, enjoying the delicious aroma of his mate. His still-hard dick twitched beneath the confines of the voluminous fabric.

Smiling to himself, Miggs hung up the towel, then tied the robe's belt. He opened the door and eased from the room. Feeling the cooler temperature of the suite, he tucked his hands into the opposite sleeves, doing his best to keep in his body heat.

Miggs scrunched his toes into the thick carpet as he paused and peered around. Spotting Delanrue relaxing at the small, round, dining room table, he smiled as he swept his gaze over the man. Delanrue had his head bowed as he looked at his phone. His other hand rested on the table, his fingers wrapped around a mug.

Perhaps Delanrue felt Miggs's focus on him or maybe he scented him. Either way, Delanrue lifted his head and pinned his intense hazel-eyed gaze on him. Even as his eyes narrowed just a little, a warm gleam filled them. His lips curved a bit at the corners.

"There is something absolutely ball-tingling about seeing you in my robe," Delanrue rumbled, his voice holding a note of smugness. "So much so, that I'm damn tempted to never buy you any clothes of your own."

Miggs felt a mixture of pleasure and unease. "Um . . ." He really wasn't certain how to respond to that.

Delanrue chuckled huskily as he rose from his seat, leaving his drink behind. "*Almost*, my little mate," he told him with a wink while stalking across the living room toward him. "Come. Time for you to eat."

Pulling his arms out of the opposite sleeves, Miggs gripped Delanrue's hand. The warmth of the man's rough palm trickled up his arm. When they reached the table, he didn't want to let go, but he did it anyway, settling in the chair Delanrue had vacated.

"Do you like coffee, Miggs?" Delanrue asked while pulling open the oven.

"Mmm, not really," Miggs told him.

At least he hadn't felt deprived when his alpha had refused to allow him to have the beverage when he was forced into servitude. Evidently, Alpha Shaun had thought it would be some kind of punishment.

Delanrue brought a covered dish to the table and set it before him. "I think the only other beverages I have here are water and alcohol." Straightening, Delanrue rubbed the back of his neck as a wry smile curved his lips. "I don't entertain much."

For some reason, Miggs liked hearing that. Plus—"I haven't had a glass of wine in years."

When Delanrue's smile morphed into a grin, Miggs knew he'd made the right choice . . . even if whatever wine his mate had on hand sucked.

Delanrue removed the cover from the dish, revealing a wealth of fragrant foods.

As his mate moved away from the table, Miggs found his attention riveted to the food before him. There were several strips of bacon as well as sausage links. A pile of fried potatoes filled part of the plate. The eggs looked cooked over-easy to perfection. There was even a heavily buttered English muffin.

Unable to resist the grumbling of his hungry stomach, or the way his mouth watered, Miggs picked up one of the English muffin halves. He pressed it against the egg, breaking the dome. The yolk spilled from the cooked white portion, and Miggs soaked some up with the muffin.

Miggs took a big bite and moaned when the flavor of the toasted bread soaked in warm yolk hit his tongue. For a few seconds, he closed his eyes and just savored the taste. Then his control broke.

Snapping open his eyelids, Miggs soaked up some more yolk and ate another bite. He finished the English muffin half in three bites. Then he picked up a slice of bacon and shoved half of the salted pork goodness into his mouth.

A moment later, a fork appeared next to his plate, followed by a glass of wine.

Yanking his focus away from the delectable meal, Miggs looked up at Delanrue. No censure was in his gaze as he met his eyes and smiled while placing a bottle of ketchup on the table, too. Before Miggs could come up with something to say, Delanrue rounded the table and stopped next to his chair and bent down.

Miggs barely managed to hold in a squeak of surprise when Delanrue lifted him into his arms. Same as in the interrogation room, the huge man sat, then placed Miggs on his lap. After cuddling Miggs to his chest, he grabbed a sausage link and held it to Miggs's lips.

Obeying the silent command, Miggs opened his mouth and took a bite of the juicy link.

Delanrue smiled, his hazel eyes gleaming with pleasure. "When I took your hand, I realized how cold you were," he told him as he continued to feed Miggs the rest of the sausage. "This way, I can help keep you warm while providing for you."

Nodding a little, Miggs swallowed his food. "Have you always been the one taking care of others? Like a little brother or sister or something?"

Miggs figured he needed to know a little about Delanrue before they discussed bonding.

Picking up the fork, Delanrue hummed, his eyes narrowing. His expression turned a little vacant, as if he were deep in thought. Even as he did that, he scooped up some of the yolk-covered egg white before stabbing a couple of pieces of crispy potatoes.

"I suppose you could say that," Delanrue told him, lifting the fork to Miggs's lips. When he'd dutifully accepted the food into his mouth, his mate continued. "I have two brothers. Both younger. Dane and Dakota respectively." As Delanrue prepared another forkful, he asked, "Would you like some ketchup?"

"Just for the potatoes, please," Miggs replied. "I don't like ketchup on my over-easy eggs. Only on scrambled ones . . . if there's cheese." Upon seeing Delanrue nod thoughtfully, clearly tucking that information away for future reference, before accepting the next bite of food, Miggs hurried and admitted, "I don't like scrambled eggs without cheese."

"Any particular kind of cheese you prefer?" Delanrue asked while putting down the fork. He grabbed the ketchup bottle and created a pool on part of the plate that wasn't near Miggs's eggs.

Miggs shrugged. "I've always just bought a block of medium cheddar or that bag of pre-shredded cheese that has a couple of different kinds in it." He searched his memory, remembering. "Um, I think it's a taco blend or something like that."

Delanrue was already nodding. "If you're interested, we can try other things," he told him as he handed him the wine. "Let me know if you like it."

At least Delanrue didn't try to help him sip it.

Miggs knew *that* would have been taking the whole caring for and feeding thing too far, and refusing could have turned things awkward. Of course, if that would have happened, maybe his arousal would have waned. As it was, sitting on Delanrue's lap, warm and comfortable, enjoying not just the food but the rich aroma of his mate, Miggs's body was in some serious need.

Taking a small sip of the wine, Miggs swallowed quickly to clear his palate. He waited a heartbeat, then took a larger mouthful, which allowed him a much better taste. The dark liquid had a hint of a bite, but the robust flavor quickly mellowed it.

"It's good," Miggs claimed before drinking some more. "Thank you."

Delanrue smiled faintly, having a forkful of potatoes dipped in a bit of ketchup on hand. "Glad you like it." As he eased the food into Miggs's mouth, he told him, "And to finish answering your question, I guess I do have a caregiver gene, but only to my brothers . . . and now you." Smirking,

Delanrue told him, "Everyone else probably thinks I'm a cold, heartless asshole."

Miggs couldn't imagine it, but he didn't say that. His mate's scent told him the big shifter spoke the truth. Fortunately, Delanrue didn't make him come up with a response.

"Anyway, after my parents died young, I took on the role of provider for my brothers," Delanrue admitted. "I was always big with a dominant animal, and as long as I stayed out of the alpha and the inner circle's way, no one messed with us." Growling softly, Delanrue grumbled, "Until Dakota turned eighteen and one of the lower enforcers decided he wanted Dakota's cherry, if you get my meaning."

Miggs cringed. "Ugh," he mumbled around his mouthful of food. "We had one of them in our muddle. When Alpha Shaun found out, he banished him."

"Wish ours had," Delanrue replied with a growl in his voice. "But he was a dumb fuck even if he was strong."

The way Delanrue's lips curved into a hard smile as his hazel eyes took on a glacial glint made Miggs appreciate that the man was his mate.

*That means he'll never direct that look at me . . . right?*

Miggs surely hoped so.

When Delanrue began rubbing his cheek against his neck, whispering words of reassurance, Miggs realized he hadn't kept his thoughts to himself.

"You're my mate, Miggs," Delanrue purred softly. "I'll always put you first. Protect you. Care for you."

Nodding, Miggs whispered, "Sorry. Just had some bad experiences with, um, those kinds of expressions." He lifted his hand and touched Delanrue's lips, stopping him from responding so he could reassure him. "I know you'll never use your size and strength against me. Fate says we're perfect complements, so she would never give me to someone who would do that." Miggs believed that with all his heart, and he smiled warmly at his mate, even though there was still an angry tightness around his eyes. "I'll just need a little time to control certain automatic reactions."

Delanrue's cheeks darkened just a smidge as he nodded slowly. "Who in your muddle?" he asked gruffly.

Miggs knew exactly what Delanrue meant, and he didn't pretend otherwise. "My father. Beta Koin."

Growling under his breath, Delanrue took a long deep breath. "Bastard," he snarled.

Then Delanrue tucked his face against Miggs's neck and inhaled slowly. He instinctively tilted his head, offering the bigger shifter more room. When Delanrue let out the breath on a soft groan, obviously reacting to the move, his warm breath caused the hairs on Miggs's neck to stand on end.

The warmth spread swiftly throughout the rest of his body, too. His dick flexed beneath his bathrobe, and he shifted restlessly. When Delanrue exhaled a second time, he even felt a bead of pre-cum bubble up from his slit.

Delanrue groaned softly against his flesh, causing even more goose bumps to break out on Miggs's skin.

Miggs barely managed to hold in a moan of his own by trapping his bottom lip between his teeth.

"You smell fantastic," Delanrue growled softly. "The scent of your arousal—" He cut off his sentence on a hum. "Delicious."

Tightening the arm around Miggs's waist, Delanrue slid his fingers between the folds.

Anticipation ratcheted through Miggs, and his stomach tightened for a new reason. When Delanrue skimmed his fingers across the flesh of his belly, Miggs shuddered. His breath caught in his chest, and he could no longer stop his whimper of need.

"Oh, my sweet little mate," Delanrue purred into his ear. "I wish to take care of all your needs." As he spoke, he skimmed his fingertips down his abdominals. When the backs of his digits slid across the crown of Miggs's erection, drawing a gasp of pleasure from him, Delanrue rumbled, "*All your needs.*"

Then Delanrue began a soft, teasing touch to his erection, skimming up and down, up and down, with just the backs of his fingers.

After the second pass, Miggs whined, "D-Del."

"Anything you want, little mate," Delanrue murmured into his ear. Then he nipped at his lobe before adding, "After you finish eating."

Then, to Miggs's utter shock, Delanrue stabbed the fork into more potatoes, coated them with ketchup, and brought it to his lips.

Miggs gaped, and Delanrue took advantage, sliding the fork inside.

*Does he really expect me to eat while he's fondling my dick?*

As Miggs chewed, Delanrue continued to touch him . . . while scooping up some eggs.

*Holy shit! He does.*

# CHAPTER FIVE

Touching his mate was better than anything Del had ever imagined—so freeing. The sensation of Miggs's skin beneath his fingers—exquisite.

Del couldn't wait to feel more, to feel everything.

First, however, he needed to finish helping his mate eat.

To do that, Del needed a distraction from the smooth skin beneath his touch. He knew just what would do it, too. As much as he hated thinking about his birth pack, he decided to share the rest of his story.

*Better it comes from me than some warped version from someone else.*

"I had a couple of friends in the herd, and one of them let me know of Enforcer Bandin's plans for Dakota," Del told Miggs. When he saw his mate's eyes widen, he met his gaze with a serious one of his own. "It didn't take a genius to figure out where Bandin planned to corner my brother. When he walked home from his part-time job, he always went through a secluded bit of the forest." Smiling wryly, Del explained, "Even at eighteen, a komodo dragon shifter is still the baddest thing in the forest, so we never feared that animals would mess with us."

Having just swallowed, Miggs murmured, "Is that what you are? A komodo dragon?"

Realizing he'd forgotten to share something so elemental, he nodded. "I am. My brothers and I are all komodo dragon shifters. My pack alpha didn't believe in inter-species matings."

Miggs nodded as he allowed Del to feed him the last bite of sausage link.

Del watched him chew the food he'd provided for a few seconds while skimming his fingertips along the soft skin of his inner thigh. When Miggs moaned softly and moved his legs wider, he felt his control slipping. He desperately wanted to untie the robe's belt, spread the fabric, and bare his mate to his gaze.

Only knowing that would be the end of question and answer time, not to mention Miggs getting to eat his meal, kept Del in control.

"Anyway," Del pressed on, sliding his thumb into the crease where Miggs's hip met his groin. "I convinced Beta Simms that I overheard a couple of pack-members threatening Dakota, but I didn't recognize their voices."

"Why would he believe that, since it was a lie?" Miggs asked curiously.

Del put down the fork and waggled his hand in a so-so gesture. "It was half-and-half. True if you looked at it from a certain way," he explained. "I *did* hear that someone was threatening harm to Dakota. I couldn't confirm their voices because I was hearing the news second hand." Seeing Miggs's brows furrow as he nodded thoughtfully, Del admitted, "And I covered the smell of any falsehood with the scent of the rage coursing through my system just at the idea of Bandin taking advantage of my brother. Hell, I didn't even know if Dakota was gay, at that point."

"Is he?"

Enjoying Miggs's curiosity, and the breathy quality of his voice, Del shrugged. "Bi. We all ended up admitting that to each other a couple of decades later." Picking up the last of the English muffin, he swiped it across the plate, soaking up the last of the egg yolk that had spilled onto the plate. "Anyway, I took Beta Simms to the most remote area of Dakota's walk, and we hid downwind. Imagine the beta's surprise when Bandin was the one to intercept my brother. He nearly blew it by interrupting, but the way Bandin pushed into Dakota's space must have halted him."

Recalling that day, Del felt a fresh wave of anger and injustice. "When it became apparent that Bandin was trying to force himself on Dakota, the beta *did* put a stop to it," he stated gruffly, feeding his mate the last of the food, allowing the simple act of caring for his other half to soothe him. "But not because Dakota wasn't interested."

"It was because he was a guy, right?" Miggs asked softly around his bite of food before swallowing.

Del nodded once. "Exactly right."

"Asshole," Miggs grumbled.

Nodding again, Del reached for his long-forgotten coffee cup. He lifted it and swigged back the remaining liquid, not caring that it was no longer hot. After finishing the drink, he returned the mug to the table and picked up Miggs's wine.

Handing it to Miggs, Del asked, "Do you need more food? I can make more of anything."

Miggs took a long sip of the wine as he peered at him from over the rim. After swallowing, he murmured, "No." Then he took a longer, deeper drink, finishing the glass.

Del immediately took it. The heat flushing Miggs's cheeks could be a mixture of the food, the wine, sitting on his lap, or the fact that his arousal perfumed the air. He struggled with how to ask what he wanted without sounding as if he were pressuring his forever mate.

Saving him the trouble, Miggs whispered, "Do you have any idea how difficult it was to just sit and eat?" He reached for the cloth tie that held the robe together. "You touching me? Exploring my body?"

With his hand still beneath the fabric, Del slid his thumb into Miggs's pubic hair. His callouses caught on the crinkly hair, and he knew the move would cause the hair to tug at the sensitive skin of Miggs's groin. The move also caused the hairs on his arm to stand on end, and he struggled to catch his own breath.

Del stared at where Miggs was oh-so-slowly untying the knot. For the first time in his life, his brain short-circuited, and he couldn't get words past his lips, so he just shook his head. All his focus remained riveted on Miggs's nimble fingers.

"Well, it's making me think selfish thoughts," Miggs admitted on a whisper. "I want more of your hands on me, but I don't know if that's a good idea."

The uncertainty bleeding into Miggs's tone and scent punctured Del's haze of lust. He snapped his focus to his mate's face and noticed the way his brows were furrowed in concern. How Miggs nibbled his bottom lip caused a desire to replace his mate's teeth with his own.

Jerking his attention upward, Del met Miggs's worried brown eyes. "What could possibly be selfish about your mate exploring your body?" he asked, finally finding his tongue.

"We probably shouldn't bond until my name is cleared," Miggs told him, obviously trying to be the voice of reason. "What if somehow my alpha makes the charges about me killing Kenny stick? What if I'm put to death for being rogue? I can't handle the idea of something happening to you because of my past, my muddle. I—"

"Enough," Del snarled, possessive anger and desire swimming through his veins in equal measure. "Nothing will *ever* happen to you," he declared. Cupping Miggs's jaw, Del tipped his head, forcing him to meet his gaze squarely. "I won't allow it. I will kill Alpha Shaun myself before I allow him and his lies to take you away from me."

Miggs's eyes widened, and he gasped. "Y-You shouldn't say such things," he mumbled. "What if someone hears?"

Del snorted as he shook his head. "Who gives a fuck?" he

replied bluntly. "We know he's lying, and we'll prove it." Dipping his head, he angled his lips toward Miggs's. "Tell me now if you don't want to bond with me, Miggs." Then Del warned, "If you have a reason other than fear for my safety, that is, because I want you." To emphasize his point, he shifted his hips, allowing his erection to press against Miggs's delectable bottom more firmly. "You're mine, and I'm yours. I've been waiting for you for almost two centuries, and now, Fate has brought you to me. I don't want to wait a second longer."

*So much for not pressuring my mate. Oh well. I'll make it up to him.*

With that thought in mind, Del sealed his mouth over Miggs's. He dipped his tongue into his unsuspecting mate's mouth, taking advantage. Delving deep, he relished the flavors that burst across his tongue — wine, food, and something all Miggs's own.

*Delicious.*

Del lapped at Miggs's tongue, entreating him to join in the kiss. Sliding the hand on his mate's jaw back a little, he threaded his fingers into his still-damp hair. He teased at the nape of his neck as he tipped his head back a little, allowing him more access.

To Del's pleasure, he felt Miggs's tongue slide against his own. He gripped Del's wrist, digging in his nails. He used the hold to press harder against Del's lips, lapping and joining in the kiss.

Reveling in the tongue-play, Del allowed Miggs to lead for several seconds. He welcomed his mate's appendage into his mouth. Sealing his lips around it, he suckled gently, hoping to soon do the same thing to his little shifter's cock.

The fresh flood of Miggs's arousal perfumed the air, and Miggs fed Del a moan.

Growling in response, Del took over the kiss. He ravished his mate's mouth. Mapping him, teasing over his teeth and tongue, he learned what made him whimper and what made him moan.

Capturing those sounds, Del felt his body's thrum of need intensify. He cupped Miggs's erection beneath the robe and swiped his thumb over his crown. Pleasure filled him upon finding the flared head wet from pre-cum.

When Miggs's dick twitched in his hand, he broke the kiss. Peering into his mate's lust-glazed eyes, he began a smooth jacking. He relished the pink glow of his little shifter's cheeks, delighting in how that same color flowed down his neck to his chest, revealed by the gaping bathrobe.

Wanting to see more, to see everything, Del no longer saw a reason to deny his need. He moved his hand to the ties that Miggs's own fingers had abandoned in favor of gripping his arm. After making quick work of the cloth, Del opened the flaps, baring his small gorgeous mate to his gaze.

"Exquisite," Del rumbled, taking in the perfect view — his needy aroused mate sprawled across his lap. Resting his hand on Miggs's slender hip, he began rocking his hips in counter-point of each downward stroke to his mate's dick. The pressure sent delicious tingles to his balls, and he knew it wouldn't be long before he was unloading in his jeans like an untried youth.

Still, Del didn't stop.

Del was too focused on Miggs's need. His breathy whimpers were music to his ears. The way his hands dug into his forearms and his feet were locked around his calves, allowing him to rock his hips, was a heady sight to behold. His new and forever lover taking pleasure from Del's ministrations drove him onward.

With his goal of seeing the lovely erection in his hand spray pearly-white seed all over Miggs's chest, Del began teasing over his ball sack with each down-stroke. On the up-stroke, he swiped his thumb over his mate's crown. The shaft in his hand twitched pleasantly, and the balls he fondled visually tightened.

"Yesss," Del hissed. Lowering his head, he pressed a kiss to Miggs's flesh where his neck met his shoulder, the place where he longed to bite. "Do it," he urged. "Show me how much you love my touch."

Then Del wrapped his lips around the flesh and sucked . . . hard.

Miggs cried out his pleasure, bucking in his hold. His body shuddered in Del's arms, and his nails bit into his flesh.

As Del watched, satisfaction flooding him, the cock in his grip pulsed. Cum spurted from the gaping slit. As the seed splattered over Miggs's slender torso, the scent of his spend flooded Del's nostrils.

Del's teeth elongated, his komodo dragon urging him to bite. While he wanted to do just that, he planned to do it with his dick in Miggs's beautiful ass. Lifting his head, he arched his neck and released his control on his own balls.

Groaning with pleasure, Del relished the waves of endorphins as his orgasm washed over him. He moaned Miggs's name as his aching shaft poured burst after burst of seed into his crotch. Returning his face to the crook of Miggs's neck, Del inhaled the scent of his mate, his seed, and contentment.

*So damn good.*

After several minutes, where the sounds of their heavy breaths were the only noise in the room, Del pressed another kiss to Miggs's neck. When he lifted his head, he smiled. While he hadn't bitten his mate, he had definitely worked up a mark.

"The way you respond to me," Del murmured, finally releasing the semi-soft prick in his hand. "Perfect."

"Not perfect," Miggs mumbled, his words just a little thick.

"Perfect for me," Del countered, sliding his left arm under Miggs's legs as he rocked forward. As he rose to his feet, he added, "And that means, yes, you're perfect."

Enjoying the way Miggs clung to him, Del carried his mate through the doorway and into the bedroom.

*Dishes can wait.*

"I guess that means you're perfect for me, too," Miggs murmured.

Placing Miggs in the center of his bed, Del grinned down at him. "I'll certainly strive to be," he promised as he grabbed the hem of his shirt. Yanking it over his head and tossing it to the floor, he could barely tear his gaze from the sight of his mate sprawled on his bed. His cock ached anew, having only softened a smidge after his release. As Del unbuttoned and removed his jeans, he offered, "My mate, tell me now if you don't want to be claimed. Otherwise . . ."

Gripping his shaft in one hand, Del fished the lube from his nightstand with the other. He tossed it on the bed, following that up by crawling onto it. Resting back on his calves between his little shifter's spread legs, Del waited.

Miggs's silence tested Del's patience, but he refused to push his mate any more than he already was. He needed the words. He needed his mate to tell him this was okay.

Slowly, Miggs removed his arms from the bathrobe. Then he lifted them, reaching for Del.

Del levered forward, taking each of Miggs's hands with his own. Sprawling forward, he moved their coupled hands above his mate's head. He rested his weight on his forearms, unwilling to crush his much smaller mate.

After pecking a kiss to Miggs's lips, Del stared into his sweetheart's deep brown eyes. He saw the searching look on his mate's face as the other shifter swept his gaze over him over and over. Del made certain his surety filled his features, letting Miggs know without words that he had complete faith in their pairing.

They would handle anything thrown at them—one way or another.

Finally, Miggs nodded once.

To Del's relief, he also spoke.

"I want to be yours, Del," Miggs whispered. "More than anything."

Hearing a hitch in Miggs's voice, Del waited, and his patience was rewarded.

"If you're sure, too."

Del smiled down at his mate. With a squeeze of his hands, he told him, "I have never been surer of anything, Miggs. You are my mate, my heart and soul, my forever." While Del had never considered himself a very eloquent man to use flowery words, he wouldn't deny his mate the truth. "With us standing side by side, we will prevail over any odds."

After watching the problems beaten by some of his fellow enforcers and the councilmen, Del believed that with all his heart.

"Claim me."

His mate's simple words filled Del with a joy that he'd never before felt.

"With pleasure." Then Del lowered his head and captured Miggs's lips once more.

# CHAPTER SIX

Miggs had never imagined how it could feel to be needed by another so very much. He saw it with every look in Delanrue's eyes. He felt it in every touch the huge man bestowed upon him.

Even though it would be so easy for the much larger shifter to flip him and take what he wanted, he hadn't done that. He'd asked. He'd waited. He'd listened. Then he'd reassured him with words and touch.

Now, Miggs felt as if he would go out of his ever-loving mind. When he'd agreed, asking to be claimed, he had thought Delanrue would flip him, grab the lube, and get straight to it. Miggs had been wrong.

Delanrue pressed their lips together, bestowing a slow, sweet, lingering kiss to his lips. At the same time, he released Miggs's hands. He skimmed one hand down his arm, then the other, all the while holding his formidable weight off of him while mapping his limbs.

When Delanrue's hands reached his shoulders, he broke the kiss.

Miggs peered up at Delanure, taking in the lustful heat filling his gaze as he swept it up, down, and back up his body.

Feeling a blush heat his lips, Miggs fought the urge to cover himself. Once upon a time, he'd considered himself a pretty good looking guy. That had been before he'd been little more than a slave whose food had been rationed.

Knowing his ribs showed and the muscle tone he used to have was gone, he grimaced and turned his head, fearing he would see disappointment in Delanrue's gaze. After all, the other shifter was huge. He sported broad shoulders with uber-thick muscles. Not only that, even when the man had been young, he'd bested an enforcer with his brain.

His mate was just as smart as he was strong.

*Guess there's a reason he's the head interrogator for the Shifter Council.*

"Heeeeey."

Delanrue's deep, soft croon coupled with his hand on Miggs's jaw drew his focus back to his mate's face.

"Where did you go, my mate?" Delanrue asked with furrowed brows. "Wherever it was, I don't like it."

Unable to help himself, Miggs blurted out, "Are you disappointed?"

Levering up a little, Delanrue stared at him in obvious surprise. "Disappointed?" He frowned. "In what?"

"Me?" Miggs nibbled his bottom lip. "In having me for a mate?"

Delanrue stared at him for a couple of agonizingly long heartbeats. Then his lips pressed into a thin line as he let out a slow breath through his nose. Finally, he shook his head before pinning a hard gaze on Miggs.

"You listen up, little mate," Delanrue ordered, a definite growl in his voice. For an instant, the pupils of his eyes flicked to vertical, revealing his animal, before he blinked and they returned to human. "I don't know what shit is going on in that brain of yours, and I'm not very good at platitudes, so listen up." Delanrue threaded the fingers of his left hand into Miggs's hair, using the hold to keep him from turning or ducking his head. "Midget Suvergy, you are my mate, and I am so fucking happy to have found you. I feel like the luckiest goddamned shifter on the planet just because you're lying in my bed, letting me hold you and touch you. Soon, I'm gonna sink my aching cock into your sweet little ass, fill you up with my cum, and bite your neck. I'm gonna bond us for eternity."

Delanrue's hazel eyes narrowed, the orbs dominated by the green as arousal swam in their depths. "And nothing could make me any happier."

Then Delanrue dipped his head. Instead of capturing Miggs's lips, like he thought he would, he latched onto one of his nipples. Feeling the sparks of pleasure erupting across his chest, he barked a cry and arched, pressing into the bigger shifter's touch.

While Miggs figured he should have been concerned or turned off by Delanrue's crass words, nothing could have been further from the truth. Instead, his mind sang with the knowledge that his shifter felt so happy to have found him. He relished the way he cared for him, in the way he touched him. His brain began shutting down as Delanrue played his body with a skill that would have instilled jealousy if he knew he wouldn't be the recipient of it for the rest of his days.

As Delanrue worked his nub with his mouth, he rubbed one hand down his side. He traced over his ribs, then down his hip. Gripping his thigh, Delanrue pulled his leg up and to the side, opening him further.

Delanrue moved to his other nipple, and Miggs grabbed onto his shoulders, needing the hold to feel grounded. His senses sang, and his body shuddered. Goose bumps broke out on his arms and legs, and shivers racked him as he felt Delanrue feather a finger over his opening.

Miggs had no idea when Delanrue had grabbed the lube, opened it, or even poured it on his fingers. Still, he felt the slick as the shifter eased a thick digit into him. He rocked his hips, finding he enjoyed the unfamiliar stretch.

"That's the way, Miggs," Delanrue murmured, sending warm breath over his already beaded nipple. "Take pleasure from my touch."

Even as Miggs opened his mouth to reply, he could form

no actual words. The zing of Delanrue rubbing over his prostate took all thought from him. Instead, a keening moan erupted from him.

As Delanrue continued to pet Miggs's body, massage his ball sack, and fondle his throbbing shaft, Miggs hummed and shuddered. He rocked into his lover's ministrations, first one way, then another. His body felt strung so tight, that he feared he would come at any second.

"Stop fighting it, my mate," Delanrue murmured before sucking hard on his distended nub for several seconds. "I need you to come. I'm big, and this will relax you, so you can take me."

*Take him?*

Finally, that pulled Miggs out of his haze of bliss long enough to articulate a single thought.

"I-I've never done this before."

Delanrue's head popped up. Focusing on him with a hint of surprise in his eyes, he stared for an instant. Then he asked, "You've never had sex? Or had sex with a man?"

After nibbling his lip for a few seconds, Miggs knew he had to be honest. "Um, both?"

A shudder worked through Delanrue's massive body. His eyelids slid shut, and his nostrils flared. Even his fingers twitched within the confines of Miggs's body.

Concern clearing his mind a bit more, Miggs worriedly asked, "D-Del?"

Delanrue opened his eyes and smiled at him. A new light had entered his gaze. One that Miggs wasn't certain he wanted to put a name to . . . at least, not yet.

"Thank you for telling me, Miggs," Delanrue murmured huskily. "I would never have purposefully hurt you, but this does change how I intend to take you for the first time."

Miggs wasn't certain what that meant, but he found out swiftly enough. When Delanrue pulled away, he nearly panicked. He squeaked and tried to hang onto his mate's shoulders even tighter.

"Easy, my mate," Delanrue purred while rubbing his left hand down his side. At the same time, he gently pulled the fingers of his right hand out of Miggs's chute. "You're okay. I've got you."

"A-Are you upset?" Having never had a lover, Miggs didn't know how to interpret Delanrue's actions. Seeing as this was his mate, he knew he needed to be brave enough to share his feelings . . . just like Delanrue had. "Because I don't know how to please you?"

Delanrue's lips curved into a wide smile as he shook his head. "Oh, my mate." Gripping Miggs's upper arm, he urged him to a sitting position. Then he pecked a kiss to his lips. "You lying there writhing under my ministrations pleases me very, very much. I look forward to making you do it often." Then Delanrue moved one hand to Miggs's hip. "Roll over, my mate."

Confused, Miggs questioned, "Roll over?"

Even as Delanrue nodded, his brows furrowed. "It'll be easier for your first time, my mate."

"Easier?" Miggs couldn't help but parrot.

"Yes," Delanrue confirmed. "The angle makes it easier for your body to stretch so widely." As he spoke, he once again urged Miggs to roll over. While moving Miggs into the position Delanrue obviously wanted, he continued, saying, "It'll also be easier for me to find your prostate this way, too." Once Miggs was on his knees and elbows, Delanrue draped over his back and whispered into his ear, "That way, I can distract you and drive you out of your mind with pleasure."

Miggs couldn't help the shiver that worked down his spine. Even his dick jerked at his groin. Anticipation caused his gut to clench.

"O-Okay," Miggs whispered, hoping for relief soon.

"Now then," Delanrue rumbled into his ear. "I'm going to ease my fingers back into you, adding a fourth," he told him. "With you being a virgin, I want to make you as loose as possible."

Feeling his cheeks flame, Miggs knew he blushed. He suddenly felt relief that he was face-down. Nodding, he cleared his throat.

"O-Okay," he repeated, because he couldn't think of anything else to say.

Delanrue nibbled the base of his neck as he grabbed the lube. "While I'm doing that." Using his thumb, he popped the cap open. "I'm going to jack your dick until you spray all over the bathrobe."

Miggs felt as if his face were on fire even as his cock throbbed with anticipation. The bead of pre-cum that rolled across his crown pulled a whimper of need from his throat. Even his balls began to tighten, as if ready to burst right that second.

"Gods, Miggs," Delanrue purred into his ear. "I love the sounds you make. Love how your need smells." Licking at Miggs's earlobe, he whispered, "Just your smell in general. So ball-tingling."

Fortunately, Delanrue sliding his fingers back into Miggs's ass saved him from having to answer. The change in position altered the sensations, making them seem so much more intense. He barked a cry when, true to his word, Delanrue immediately teased over his prostate.

Chuckling roughly, Delanrue rubbed his cheek against Miggs's nape. "Love those sounds. Show me more."

Then Delanrue reached under him with his free hand and gripped Miggs's dick.

Miggs groaned and thrust his hips, unable to help himself. Rocking back again, he pushed against Delanrue's embedded fingers. Once more, the sparks he recognized as his lover playing with his prostate shot up his rectum.

Losing himself to those sensations, Miggs moved faster. He pushed into Delanrue's fist only to press back onto his fingers. Each move caused more and more fire to course through his veins. His gut clenched, and sweat broke out on his brow.

Just as Delanrue whispered into his ear, "Do it. Come for me. Spray your seed. I want to smell it," Miggs felt the man ease another digit into him.

The mild burn took his breath away, but his body was too far gone. Even that hint of pain couldn't stop him from careening over the edge. His orgasm rolled through his body, the bliss-inducing endorphins roaring within him.

"Del!" Miggs cried, shuddering and jolting.

The way Delanrue gently continued to jack his dick, while teasing over his balls, kept Miggs's senses singing. His mind floated with ecstasy, his brain fuzzing out. While Miggs registered that Delanrue removed his fingers, he didn't bother to move.

He felt too good.

A second later, Miggs felt something else at his entrance.

"Push out, Miggs," Delanrue ordered.

At the same time, the pressure at Miggs's anus intensified until something much larger than Delanrue's fingers popped into his chute. When the mild burn spiked through him, his first instinct was to clench. Remembering his mate's words, as odd as they were, Miggs did his best to do that instead.

Miggs inhaled deeply as a shiver worked down his spine. Letting it out slowly, he pushed out.

"That's the way, my mate," Delanrue crooned, praising him. "Doing so good. Feel so exquisite."

Delanrue continued to whisper words of praise as he sank his dick deeper into Miggs's body. The way the big shifter ran his hands up and down Miggs's sides, played with his pubic hairs, and teased over his nut sack distracted him in the best possible ways. When Delanrue gripped his nipple and squeezed, Miggs moaned, all pain in his chute forgotten.

"Gods, Miggs," Delanrue growled, suddenly sounding strained. "You're so perfect. Fit me so beautifully." He pinched Miggs's other nipple as he rumbled, "Think we should get these pierced? They're so sensitive. Would make your body sing just by playing with them."

Even as Miggs's mind balked at the idea, the way it felt to have Delanrue play with them was quickly changing his mind. Tingles flowed down his chest, making his stomach clench. His balls warmed as his dick thickened once more.

"That's the way, my mate," Delanrue muttered. "Gods, you open so nicely for me. Such a sweet squeeze on my cock."

Miggs finally realized that Delanrue must have bottomed out at some point, for he was already easing his erection back out of his body. To his surprise, it no longer hurt, either. His body easily accommodated Delanrue's girth, and as the big shifter pulled out of him, it left Miggs with a feeling of emptiness he didn't understand.

"N-No," Miggs whined, trying to push back, to force Delanrue's dick back into his body. His lover's grip on his hip stopped him, and he trembled. "P-Please."

"I got you, Miggs," Delanrue assured.

"More," Miggs pleaded.

"Anything for you, my mate," Delanrue replied, moving to blanket his body while pushing back into him much too slowly. "Had to make sure you were ready."

Miggs sighed and arched, moving on instinct. "So ready."

Delanrue growled into Miggs's ear, "Yeah, you are," before suckling his lobe.

Then Delanrue wrapped his arm around Miggs's waist, anchoring his back to Delanrue's chest. His big lover kept his weight on his other arm even as he used his torso to press Miggs closer to the mattress. Once Miggs's chest had been pressed flush to the bathrobe, a growl from the big man vibrated the chest behind him.

"Perfect," Delanrue declared.

Then he sped up.

Miggs cried out in delight as Delanrue's cock slid over his prostate. His lover hammered into him, moving his prick in and out, in and out, at a speed Miggs never imagined was possible. Each pass dragged over his pleasure gland, sending spikes of bliss flooding his body.

To Miggs's shock, his balls began tightening once more. He shivered, fighting against it, trying to stave off another embarrassingly fast orgasm.

"Do it," Delanrue snarled into his ear. "I feel the trembles in your body, the fluttering of your chute muscles. Come. Clamp onto my dick. I want you to squeeze me so tight, to hold me within your sweet body."

Gasping, Miggs lost control, his body instantly obeying. His balls forced burst after burst of seed from him, even though he couldn't believe he had anything left after his two prior orgasms. He didn't even try to control the way his channel contracted as his gut clenched.

"Yesssss," Delanrue hissed into his ear, burying his length deep in Miggs's body.

Miggs felt him go still inside him right before the heat of Delanrue's cum warmed him from the inside out. He murmured his lover's name, relishing the unfamiliar sensation. Feeling Delanrue's teeth at his neck, Miggs tilted his head, giving his mate more room.

The flash of pain caused Miggs to gasp, but the delicious zings immediately washed it away. They flooded his balls, yanking Miggs over the ledge once again.

When black spots danced across his vision, Miggs succumbed to the blissful darkness.

# CHAPTER SEVEN

Del felt his sweet little mate's body go limp, and smug satisfaction flooded him.

*Gods, that was intense.*

Keeping his arm tight around Miggs's body, Del carefully eased them to the left. He slid that arm up and grabbed a pillow, positioning it under their heads. Then he eased his left arm under Miggs so he could continue to clutch him close.

Del grabbed the edge of the bathrobe with his right hand and began rubbing away the drying cum from their first round at the dining room table from Miggs's chest. He knew he needed to pull out, so he could clean them up properly, but he wasn't ready to leave the hot cocoon of his mate's body just yet. His dick remained hard, and he knew, given a few minutes, he would be ready to rut to completion once more.

While Del knew Miggs had been a virgin, which meant it was probably a bad idea to continue fucking, his instinct to continue to claim his mate rode him hard. He didn't know if it was because his mate was in danger or if it was because of his dominance. Hell, maybe it was because he really was an asshole.

All Del knew was that he couldn't pull out just yet.

After clearing away as much of the dried cum as possible, Del relaxed on the bed. He wrapped his big body around his much smaller lover as much as possible, doing his best to keep him warm. Rubbing his hands gently over Miggs's too-slender frame, he mapped every contour of his body that he could reach.

Never in his life had Del felt more content.

Smiling, Del buried his face in the crook of Miggs's neck. He smelled the way their combined scents heralded his claiming. His heart thudded with happiness. He knew every paranormal they came in contact with would know that Del had claimed his little guinea pig shifter.

Del couldn't believe what a difference a few hours could make. Less than four hours before, he'd been having lunch with his brother. His biggest concern had been extracting as much information from Pedro as he could manage.

Now, Del cared little for that. Instead, he only wanted to keep his mate safe. He would figure out what was going on with his lover's muddle and clear up the riff-raff.

*I can ask Lachlan for aid. I bet he and his mate would love the chance to remove another bigoted asshole from command.*

Hearing Miggs's soft moan and feeling him shift a little in his arms pulled Del away from his thoughts of the feline ex-investigator and his tom turkey mate. He lifted his head a little so he could stare at his mate's face. His lover's eyelashes fluttered a little, and Del knew the man was seconds away from waking.

Del rubbed his palm across Miggs's stomach gently, coaxing him back to the land of the living.

Miggs hummed, a smile curving his lips even before his eyes slowly opened. Turning his head, he peered at him. Then his eyes widened. In the same instant, Miggs's chute muscles clenched on Del's imbedded prick, drawing a soft groan from him.

Seeing Miggs's cheeks turning pink as the room was flooded with concern was the only reason Del didn't immediately start rutting.

"Easy, Miggs," Del murmured, nuzzling his neck. "It's okay. It's just us here." Rubbing his palm over Miggs's stomach, he added, "I won't let anything happen to you."

"I-I'm sorry."

Surprised and confused at Miggs's words, Del paused in his movements. "You have nothing to be sorry for," he told him, guessing at what had upset him. "I'm damn proud to have given you so much pleasure that you passed out from bliss."

For a second, Miggs didn't respond. "B-But . . . I left you, um, hanging."

"Hanging?" Del repeated, struggling to comprehend in his aroused state. Then it hit him—aroused. "Oh, my mate." He pecked a kiss to Miggs's nape as he tightened his arm around his waist. "You didn't. I just didn't soften right away after I came and"—Del paused, fighting his embarrassment, then finished—"I love the way your silky passage feels, so I didn't pull out." For an instant, Del thought he should do just that, but he couldn't help but ask, "Is this okay, Miggs?"

*Yep, thinkin' with my dick. Haven't done that in over a century.*

Miggs peered over his shoulder at him with wide eyes. "Y-You came, but . . . didn't want to, um, pull out of me?"

Del nodded. "Yeah. Sorry." He felt his face flush, and he couldn't remember the last time he blushed. "I'll just—"

Except, when Del began to rock his hips backward, intending to withdraw, Miggs grabbed his hip.

"Stop," Miggs whispered. A shy smile toyed around his lips. "I like that."

Relaxing again, Del pulled Miggs flush to his chest. "Do you?" he murmured, nuzzling at his mate's neck again, licking over his fresh claiming scar. "Like knowing I needed you so much?"

"Yeah," Miggs whispered. "I, um, I don't think I can get off again, but"—he paused, rubbing over Del's hip, clearly thinking about his words before finishing—"I'd like to feel you spill in me again. I like how that feels."

Del groaned, his arousal surging. "Oh, Miggs," he muttered. Unable to help himself, he began a slow rutting. "You are so fucking perfect for me." The feel of Miggs's silky walls caressing his sensitive length quickly loosened any restraint on his tongue, and Del admitted, "Gonna slide right in here so often, my mate. Love pleasuring us both."

Miggs sighed deeply as he once again gripped Del's forearms, using them as leverage. "Love how this feels, too."

"My mate," Del muttered, mouthing at his mating mark. Hearing the way Miggs moaned at his ministrations, he slowly began adjusting his thrusts at each pass. When Miggs shuddered in his arms and his whimpers filled the air, Del grinned. "Yeah, right there. Love hearing those noises."

Keeping his movements slow and steady, Del relished the hums of pleasure that filled the air. His little mate was so damn vocal. The soft moans followed by throaty grunts caused Del's own arousal to heat hotter than he'd ever experienced.

It didn't take long for Del to feel the familiar, tell-tale tingle in his balls. His stomach clenched pleasantly, and warmth trailed through his veins. He didn't try to stop his orgasm from swelling through him, the ecstasy blanketing his senses as he poured his release into his mate.

That didn't mean Del didn't plan to take his mate with him.

Elongating his canines, Del eased them into his claiming mark. He felt the skin pop just as he heard Miggs gasp. Sucking on the wound, reveling in the exquisite flavor of his mate's live-giving fluid, Del smiled around the flesh in his mouth as he felt his mate tremble in his arms.

A second later, to Del's satisfaction, he scented the aromatic perfume of his mate's cum fill the air.

*Delicious.*

Easing his teeth from Miggs's skin, Del swallowed one last time. Then he licked the mark clean, sealing it again. He kissed the scar before nuzzling his cheek against Miggs's temple.

"W-Wow," Miggs whispered breathily. "Didn't think I'd be able to come again."

Del kissed the back of Miggs's neck before telling him, "My bite will always get you off."

"Really?"

Upon hearing the surprise in Miggs's tone and scenting it in the air, Del finally eased his semi-soft prick from his mate's body. He urged his little shifter onto his back, then half-sprawled over him. Careful to keep most of his weight off the much smaller male, Del roved his gaze over Miggs's gorgeous features.

"Did your parents not tell you about fated mates, my little guinea pig?" Even in Del's dysfunctional pack, there had still been explanations of mates, fated or otherwise.

"Not really," Miggs told him. "There were some things whispered by some of the older members. I overheard how the scent of someone will smell better than anything you've smelled before, and it would almost be a compulsion to bond with her." His brows furrowed as he told him, "That was how I knew you were my Fate-given mate, although no one ever said anything about Fate paring those of the same sex." Miggs's cheeks took on a pinkish hue as he admitted, "I was a little surprised when those other guys offered their congratulations."

Del fought down his desire to growl. Instead, he shook his head and vowed, "We'll make that controlling, homophobic alpha pay."

Cocking his head, Miggs rubbed up and down Del's arms. "But how? He's the alpha. His word in the muddle is law."

"That doesn't give him the authority to subjugate members, kill members, or steal from members," Del countered, even though he knew so very many alphas did all those things. "Alphas are supposed to be caring for, helping, aiding, and guiding their members."

From Miggs's obvious disbelief, Del knew that hadn't been his sweet little mate's experience. That was okay. He would make certain Miggs's life contained nothing but happiness from this day forward.

*Okay. So I'll do my damnedest, anyway.*

Del would be the first to confirm that life wasn't all rainbows and unicorns all the time.

"Not all packs are like the ones we grew up in," Del told his mate. "I'll have to introduce you to some of the good alphas sometime."

As a council interrogator, Del had access to just about every Shifter Council file save the most classified. He could easily find good alpha packs in the area. Del would have to show his mate that not all alphas were like Alpha Shaun.

*Just too many of them.*

While Miggs's expression appeared a little hesitant, he still nodded.

Del heard the chime of his phone and frowned. Turning his head, he swept his gaze over the floor. He spotted his jeans not too far away, just far enough where he had to roll off his mate to be able to reach them.

Grumbling under his breath, Del eased sideways. He leaned off the bed and snagged his belt. Lifting them, he fished his phone from his pocket before dropping the soiled fabric back to the floor.

Rolling back to face Miggs, Del flopped his leg over his mate's thighs. He rested on his side, facing the small shifter, as he unlocked the device. Opening the message, he snorted and rolled his eyes.

"Is everything okay?"

Del heard the uncertainty in Miggs's tone and felt the way he snuggled against him, clearly seeking comfort — or maybe warmth. Easing his arm under his man, he turned his body. Then he used the hold to roll them, urging Miggs to drape over his larger body.

That also allowed Del to hold his phone's screen in Miggs's line of sight. "Just my brother reminding me that even finding my mate is not an excuse for missing his Christmas party."

Miggs glanced from the phone, to Del's face, back to the phone, and back again. With wide eyes, the scent of his shock filling the air, Miggs whispered, "You told your brother about me?"

"Of course," Del replied. It was his turn to feel confused. "Dakota and Dane are my only family. They'll be happy for us."

Miggs opened his mouth, then closed it again.

Once more, Del found himself waiting for his mate to put his thoughts in order.

Finally, Miggs whispered, "What if I get you in trouble or injured?"

Del fought back his urge to sigh. "My mate," he murmured softly, putting down his phone so he could thread those fingers through his lover's hair. "I love that you are so worried about my welfare. Really, but" — Del waggled his eyebrows — "if you haven't noticed, I'm a big, badass enforcer for the council. There's no way I could be hurt, even if the alpha attacked me with his entire muddle."

Just the idea of a couple of dozen guinea pigs attacking him caused a snort to erupt from Del's lips.

Miggs shook his head, his eyes widening. "But that's not how he would come at you," he warned. "He'd try to blackmail you or shoot you or make up something about you." Before nibbling his bottom lip, Miggs finished, "Like he's doing to me."

Cradling Miggs's jaw, Del used his thumb to gently tug his mate's abused lip from between his teeth. "I take your warning seriously," he told his mate. "That's why Head Enforcer Mycroft is putting an investigator to discreetly look into your *ex*-alpha's activities." Gently massaging Miggs's nape in an effort to soothe, Del told him, "He won't be able to bring trouble to us without causing even more for himself."

Miggs cocked his head. "*Ex*-alpha?"

Del nodded, smiling. "Caught that? Good."

"But why ex?"

"Because you're mated with a representative of the Shifter Council," Del explained. "That means you're under the council's jurisdiction now . . . and their protection."

"Wow!"

Before Del could say anything else, his phone chimed again. Looking at the device, he scoffed. Then Del returned his attention to Miggs.

"Guess it's time to clean up. We have a party to get to."

Miggs gaped. "A party?"

"Yep." Del eased his hold so he could swing from the bed. Then he helped his more-than-a-little uncoordinated mate from the bed. "Here's something else that would happen if I ended up hurt or in trouble."

As Miggs allowed him to be guided back into the shower, he asked, "What's that?"

Del grinned as he picked up a fresh washcloth. "My brothers would totally try to kick my ass if I got into trouble and hadn't asked for their help in the first place."

Miggs stared at him wide-eyed, clearly not getting it.

As Del cleaned his mate, he knew that was okay.

*Once Miggs meets my brothers, he'll understand.*

# CHAPTER EIGHT

M iggs wanted to hide behind Del—his mate had encouraged him to call him that on the ride over—but he didn't want to embarrass his mate, either. That didn't stop him from clinging tightly to his shifter's hand, so very pleased that the man had offered it to hold.

"Try to relax, my sweet little mate," Del rumbled softly, a reassuring smile on his lips as he guided him up the walkway. "You are my mate. You will be welcomed." Then his brows furrowed. "Try to keep in mind, the welcome may be a little boisterous."

"B-Boisterous?" Miggs glanced at the closed door nervously. "What do you mean?"

Del winked as he rolled his shoulder in a half-shrug. "I'm the first of us to find our mate, so they'll be excited." He scoffed before adding, "And maybe a little jealous. They may razz you a bit about trying to steal you from me, and I may threaten to disembowel them, but it's all in good fun." Then he pointed at the doorknob with the index finger of the hand carrying a six-pack of bottled beer. "Open that, would ya, please, sweet?"

"Disembowel?" Miggs muttered as he grasped the indicated knob and turned. "Gross."

Chuckling, Del told him, "You'll get used to us."

"My brother is laughing!" a voice nearly as deep, but far less serious, called from within. "Who could create such a response?" A second later, the already open door was yanked wide, and a man who resembled Del appeared. "Del! You made it." Then he focused on Miggs, and a cheeky grin creased his lips. "And who might you be, cutie?"

Before Miggs managed to untie his tongue, Del answered for him. "This is Miggs, as you well know." He released Miggs's hand, only to immediately wrap that arm around Miggs's waist and tuck him against his side. "But you already knew that, Dane. Get your own mate."

The man—Dane, the older-younger brother—grinned broadly. "Gods, my brother's mated." Then he leaned out the door and inhaled deeply. Straightening, his grin turned cheeky as he turned his head and hollered to someone behind him. "I win the bet. They're mated. I told you Del wouldn't wait."

"What the fuck?" hollered another voice. Then the thud of footsteps sounded through the home and another man—also definitely a brother, which would make him Dakota—rushed down the hallway toward them. "Damn it, Del! After talking to you on the phone, I could have sworn you were gonna be a gentleman and at least give the man a day."

"You fuckers," Del grumbled, shaking his head, although his scent was filled with amusement. Then Del used his six-pack-filled hand to shove Dane out of the way. "Move it, Dane. It's not that warm out here, and you're acting like an ass."

"No different than normal when it's just us," Dane countered, stepping backward. His smile remained in place as he held out his hand to Miggs. "I'm Dane." With an eyebrow waggle, he added, "The handsome brother."

Miggs hesitated an instant, then girded up his courage and took the other shifter's hand. To his surprise, the bigger male didn't do anything other than offer a friendly handshake. He didn't even squeeze in dominance or force him to drop his gaze in submission.

After releasing him, Dane closed the door behind them.

"You know where the food is, man." He chuckled as he added, "And since you've already been putting your man to work, best go get your little cutie plenty of it."

Del growled softly as he scowled over his shoulder at Dane. "I'm taking damn good care of my mate's needs, ass-hole."

Dane tipped his head back and laughed, completely unperturbed by Del's reply.

Before Miggs could manage to wrap his mind around the interaction, Dakota stepped in front of them, holding out his hand. "I'm Dakota." With a cheeky grin, he told him, "And if Dane is the handsome brother, that means *I'm* the charming one."

Del scoffed, rolling his eyes.

Miggs took Dakota's hand. Instead of a quick release, Dakota held on and stepped close. He didn't so much as tower over him, but bend and draw close as if preparing for an intimate conversation . . . which he did.

Whispering in Miggs's ear—which was ridiculous since they were all shifters and would be able to hear him—Dakota asked, "Are you certain you wouldn't enjoy someone with a softer touch, Miggs?" He rubbed his thumb over the back of his hand while adding, "I know what a roughneck my brother can be sometimes."

Although Miggs didn't necessarily know what a roughneck was, the context told him enough. Even as Del growled from beside him, he tugged his hand free from the brother's grip. With his other hand, Miggs pressed his palm against Dakota's chest and pushed.

Praying that his mate hadn't been exaggerating that their interactions were all in good, brotherly fun—after all, Miggs didn't have any brothers—he stated, "Trust me. Del is doing a fantastic job of offering soft touches." He forced a smirk as he added, "Besides, I don't think you could handle someone like me."

Miggs watched both Dane and Dakota exchange a look. Their brows ratcheted high on their foreheads. Out of the corner of Miggs's eye, he saw the corner of Del's lips twitch.

Then Dakota broke into laughter as Dane slapped Del on the back of his shoulder. "Congrats, Del." He grinned at Miggs. "Welcome to the family, Miggs. You ever need anything"—he wrapped his arm around the back of Dakota's head in a half-headlock thing—"you let us know." Dane's eyes narrowed as he told him, "We watch out for family, and you're our brother's mate. That makes you family."

Dakota nodded from the uncomfortable-looking hold. "Don't forget that, Miggs. Not ever."

Relief filling him, Miggs nodded. "Thank you."

Dane released Dakota and moved past them. "Come on. I'll introduce you to everyone."

Miggs froze as he watched the brothers disappear down the hall and around a corner. "There are others here?"

Del nodded. "This is Dakota's Christmas party, so there are a few shifters and their mates." He tipped his head to the side and sniffed at the area. "From Dane's scent, I'm guessing the date with some female didn't work out. Probably for the best." Shaking his head, Del urged Miggs forward, guiding him down the hall after the brothers. "That means it'll probably be a couple of councilmen, a few enforcers, plus the mates of those who have them."

*Holy shit!*

An hour later, Miggs's mind reeled. He'd been introduced to a *lot* of people, and he feared he wouldn't remember half of them. Still, everyone had been friendly and welcoming, which had definitely been a change from his muddle.

With a glass of wine in hand, Miggs sat on one of the love seats. He could see Del a little ways across the room. His mate faced him, but he seemed to have his attention on the man he spoke with.

If Miggs wasn't mistaken—which was possible, really—the man Del spoke with was a councilman named—

*Dang it. Who is he again?*

"That's Councilman Regales Colearian, grizzly shifter," stated a man as he sat down beside Miggs. He sighed as he relaxed against the cushions. With a smile, the guy—a human, judging by his scent—added, "I'm his mate, Theo, by the way."

Miggs nodded slowly, doing his best to store that information away for later. "Nice to meet you . . . again."

Theo grinned a second before sobering. "I've been where you are, Miggs. Trust me." Shaking his head, he peered around the room. "It'll all come together before too long, but nobody here will give you grief if you need to ask for their name again."

Even as Miggs nodded, he wasn't certain he would feel comfortable doing that. His father was the beta of his muddle—*ex-muddle*—and had told him time and again to always remember names the first time. *Having to ask shows weakness.*

Casting about for a topic of conversation, Miggs decided to go with, "So, um, how long have you been mated with the councilman?" Hopefully, that was safe.

Humming, Theo cocked his head. "Oh, over three years now." The human scoffed softly. "Time does fly. It feels like only yesterday I was telling the man I wasn't gay or interested."

Miggs gasped. "You told a councilman no?"

Theo shrugged. "Sure."

"Did you not know who he was?" Then Miggs had another idea. "Oh, I bet you needed to learn about the paranormal world to understand why you were suddenly drawn to a man. Right?"

Miggs had seen human women brought into his muddle,

and they'd always had quite a bit of adjusting to do to understand their muddle's culture.

Theo barked a laugh even as he shook his head. "Naw, I knew who he was, and I've known about the paranormal since I was young," he claimed before taking a sip of his beer. Evidently, Miggs didn't hide his shock nearly well enough, for after he'd swallowed, Theo told him, "My mother is a witch. She's even come out to vet Regales after we mated." Theo must have been thinking about something amusing, for he added, "That was fun."

Finally finding his tongue, Miggs blurted out, "If you knew about shifters, how could you deny your mate?"

Sobering, Theo curved his lips into a sad smile. "Not everything is cut and dried, Miggs." Then his eyes narrowed. "Not like how your alpha is an asshole with his fingers in too many pies for his own good."

Miggs reeled at the subject change for a few seconds. Then he realized he'd asked a personal question that he really had no right to. He had no right to know details of a councilman and his human's mating.

Focusing on what Theo had just told him, Miggs couldn't help but correct, "*Ex*-alpha." When he saw Theo arch one brow in silent question, he said, "That's what Del told me. That Shaun is no longer my alpha." Then Miggs took a sip of his wine to stop himself from saying more.

Theo nodded a few times. "Yeah. I can see that."

After Miggs had swallowed, he reached over and picked up the plate of cookies, brownies, and meat-filled finger foods that Del had prepared for him. "Do you want anything?" he offered, holding it out to Theo.

Peering at the offerings, Theo hummed. "Yum. Thanks." Then he took a small chocolate-peanut butter bar. "Good thing bonding with a shifter helped speed up my metabolism, or I'd be paying for how many of these I've eaten tonight."

With an appreciative grunt, he bit the treat in half.

Miggs had eaten a few of them, too, so he completely understood. They were delicious. After placing the plate between them, he chose a tiny baked bread pocket filled with spicy Italian sausage.

"Um, what did you mean?" Miggs asked slowly. Before taking a bite, he clarified, "About Alpha Shaun and pies?"

"Ah, human expression," Theo muttered around his food. Then he swallowed twice and licked his lips. Finally, he told him, "What I mean is, he has connections to a variety of shady people. He's had a number of suspicious-looking payments show up in his account over the last few years." Theo's eyes narrowed. "And those are not the payments he's receiving for selling his enforcers and trackers as hired muscle to gangs in town."

Miggs just stared in shock.

"Surprised you, I see," Theo stated with a nod and a small smile. "Glad to know, actually." After another sip of his beer, Theo took a pink-icing-topped sugar cookie from the plate. "It seems there's something to do with a pet store, too, but I'm still trying to wrap my brain around that one."

"Pet store?"

Looking up . . . and up . . . Miggs found himself staring at a huge man with a bald head and a bushy beard. The guy had piercing brown eyes and heavy brows. His limbs were thick with muscle, although he had a slight indication of the beginning of love handles.

Link, Miggs's brain supplied.

"Yeah, Link," Theo replied, revealing he obviously knew the shifter, too. "A pet store in Savannah."

Rubbing his hand over his big beard, Link narrowed his eyes. "I recently came across a police report filed about a theft at a pet store, but the security footage appeared to have been corrupted."

Miggs didn't know what that meant, but Theo seemed to understand.

"Corrupted how?" the human asked.

"Well, the file says some articles of clothing had been stolen," Link told them, tapping his forefinger on his beer. "But the footage was altered to make it look like a guinea pig climbed out of its cage, turned into a human, stole the clothes, then disappeared out the back door, setting off the alarm."

Gaping, Miggs could only shake his head.

Theo groaned. "Fuck. He's not really so stupid as to sell his muddle-members to pet stores, is he?"

Shrugging one massive shoulder, Link rumbled, "It'd be a good way to get rid of unwanted members. If they get caught, he claims they went rogue, and the member is the one who gets in trouble for putting the secret of paranormals in jeopardy."

*Oh gods. Could Alpha Shaun really be doing that?*

Miggs had heard of several shifters disappearing, some of them even before he'd become a slave.

"Miggs? Little mate?" Del knelt before him, telling him he'd been out of it longer than he'd realized. "Come here."

A second later, Miggs was lifted in the air. Del settled in his seat, and he was placed on his lap. Not too proud to take advantage, Miggs cuddled into his huge mate's chest.

"What if Alpha Shaun is selling his members?" Miggs whispered. "Some have disappeared."

Link settled in a nearby chair, as did Councilman Colearian.

"Tell us everything," Theo urged.

With Del's encouragement, Miggs shared everything he'd noticed over the several years he'd been a slave. At the time, most of the interactions hadn't seemed significant.

Armed with the new information about Alpha Shaun's activities, Miggs began to see things differently.

His ex-alpha had been culling their members and making

money in the process.

# CHAPTER NINE

Waking with Miggs in his arms should have felt awkward, but after three days, Del couldn't imagine ever waking without his mate again. Curled around his sexy little shifter made each morning wonderful. He hoped that never changed.

The sex first thing in the morning might have had something to do with how much he enjoyed it, too.

Del pressed light kisses to the top of Miggs's head as he rubbed his palms up and down his mate's slender back. With the way his lover sprawled across his chest after riding him, it allowed his half-hard prick to continue resting in his lover's channel. He relaxed in the afterglow of an epic orgasm while relishing the fact that he was still connected with Miggs.

After a few minutes of silence, Del wondered if Miggs had drifted back to sleep. It wouldn't have been the first time. His mate had had several harrowing years and was still recovering.

While it was probably too soon, Del believed that he could see a difference in Miggs's weight. His sweet shifter had an appetite, and Del loved indulging in it. He found great pleasure in all aspects of providing for him.

"I love lying on your chest," Miggs mumbled sleepily, letting Del know he was still awake. He turned his head so he could peer at him through his lashes. A shy smile that shouldn't be possible—considering Del still had his dick in his ass—curved Miggs's lips as he added, "You're always so warm, like you're my own personal bed-heater."

As Del traced over Miggs's still too-prominent ribs, he found he wasn't surprised that his shifter had trouble generating enough body heat. For the most part, his little shifter wore sweatshirts and warm pants. Del had even turned up the heat in their room, changing his own attire to lounge pants and a tank top.

"I love being your bed-heater," Del told Miggs, smiling at him. He moved a hand to Miggs's face, and he began tracing around his mate's lips — the lips he loved sampling as often as possible. Of course, due to their height differences, he would have to shift Miggs off his prick to do it right then, so he resisted. "I'll always be right here to keep you warm."

Miggs beamed at him, causing Del's heart — one so many people had called cold — to thud wildly in his chest. He knew it was too soon, but he recognized the feeling. After three days, Del already loved his sweet little mate.

*And I'll do anything to keep him right here by my side.*

With that thought in mind, Del remembered the phone call he'd received from Investigator Ryzer the evening before. He'd intended to discuss it with Miggs, but then his sexy shifter had walked out of the bathroom . . . wearing only a pair of skimpy underwear. Speaking of, he wondered where his shifter had gotten them.

"I received some news from Investigator Ryzer last night," Del told Miggs, running his fingers through his lover's short, dark hair. He loved the way it flopped into his mate's eyes when he didn't use styling gel to hold it in place. "But your sexy underwear distracted me." Upon recalling the sensual blue silk boy shorts, his fingers twitched with a renewed desire to touch. "Where did you get those, anyway?"

Miggs's cheeks flushed pink, and he nibbled his bottom lip.

Del responded by using his thumb to free the abused flesh. "Miggs," he rumbled, drawing out his mate's name. "Tell me." Scenting Miggs's unease, Del rocked his hips, pulling free of his mate's body. Then he immediately rolled them, moving Miggs to his back so he could blanket his little shifter. Sliding one hand into his mate's hair, he tugged on the soft strands gently while pecking a kiss to his lover's lips. "Nothing you say will upset me." With a wink, Del added, "I'll just want to know how I can get you some more. A *lot* more."

Miggs still sported a blush, but he now scented of happiness. "Um, your brother," he all but whispered. "Dane."

Unable to help himself, Del's jaw sagged open. "Dane?" he asked, flabbergasted. "I didn't even know he knew about my . . ." Letting his voice trail off, he shook his head in wonder.

Nodding, Miggs told him, "At the Christmas party, he pulled me aside." Miggs's cheeks turned even darker. "Um, he had a magazine that he said he'd found you looking at." His voice lowered to a whisper once more as he admitted, "Dane helped me pick out a few things, then ordered them for me."

"And he dropped them off yesterday afternoon," Del guessed, nodding. He'd seen a few pairs of sweatpants on top of the bag of clothes when his brother had dropped by, so he'd logically just assumed it was all standard clothes. "Sneaky bastard." Then Del focused on something else Miggs had told him. Grinning widely, he pinned a hungry look on his mate as his prick began to thicken once more. "Soooo . . . a *few* things, hmmm?"

"Yes," Miggs replied, smiling shyly at him.

"Oh, my little mate," Del rumbled, knowing he would never get enough of claiming Miggs as his own. "Are you going to put on a fashion show every night for me?"

"I-If you want."

"I very much want," Del declared, lowering his head, intending to kiss Miggs. The sound of an alarm made him pause. Groaning, Del released Miggs so he could reach over and grab his phone from the nightstand. "Damn it." Silencing the alarm, Del focused on Miggs again. "We have a meeting to get to. I got a little distracted last night and forgot to tell you."

As Del spoke, he eased off the bed and held his hand out to Miggs. "Come on, little mate. I'll tell you about it in the shower."

Less than forty-five minutes later, walking to the meeting room, Del wished he hadn't shared every detail with Miggs. His lover's nerves flooded the corridor, and he gripped Del's hand tightly. Still, Del would never lie to his mate, and in his book, withholding information was doing about the same thing.

Besides, Miggs needed to be prepared. After all, his father was waiting in the meeting room.

Del wasn't certain how Beta Koin had learned that Miggs was there so that was definitely one of the questions he planned to ask. Per his request, Interrogator Malone would be joining them, but that was for looks alone. Del planned to be the one to question Miggs's father.

*I will get what I want from the shifter . . . by any means necessary.*

Of course, Beta Koin thought he was there just to pick up his son.

*Boy, will he be surprised.*

Del mentally smirked.

Pausing at the door, Del turned and wrapped his arms around Miggs. He pulled his lover close and stared down at his little man. "Remember," Del stated, pinning a serious gaze on his mate. "This is my job. What I do, but you will always be safe with me. You will not be leaving with that asshole who sired you."

Miggs stared up at him for a few seconds, then nodded slowly. "I know I'm safe with you."

Anxiety that Del hadn't even been aware he carried eased

from him. After nodding, he bent and pecked Miggs's lips with a hard, possessive kiss. Then he straightened and gave his mate a tight smile.

"Let's go deal with this asshole," Del declared, narrowing his eyes. "I believe he's going to have a lot to say."

Once Miggs had nodded, Del eased one arm from his waist but kept the other securely around him. He grabbed the knob and opened the door. Pushing it open, he guided Miggs into the room. With a flick of his wrist, Del closed the door behind him.

Del swept his gaze over the room, and he spotted everyone Investigator Ryzer had told him would be there. Due to keeping his identity as discreet as possible, Ryzer himself was not there. Instead, Councilman Colearian sat at the head of the table, a couple of file folders resting in front of him. Standing a couple of feet behind the councilman's left shoulder was Enforcer Dane.

A couple of seats down from the councilman and on his left sat a man Del didn't recognize. From the shade of his brown eyes and facial features, he guessed him to be Miggs's father—Beta Koin Suvergy. The hard lines of his expression twisted into smug satisfaction when his gaze fell upon Miggs.

Del couldn't wait to wipe that expression off his face.

A dark-haired man stood behind Beta Koin's chair, and Del guessed him to be the muddle enforcer Ryzer said would be allowed in the meeting—Enforcer Omar.

To the left of the door they'd just entered stood Enforcer Germaine. There was also a door behind Beta Koin, and that one was guarded by the black panther shifter, Enforcer Gierson. The final man in the room was Interrogator Malone, and he sat at the other end of the table.

"Ah, Enforcer Delanrue. Miggs," Councilman Colearian greeted with a nod. "Thank you for joining us. Some questions have arisen that need clarification."

"Of course, Councilman," Del responded with a respectful dip of his chin. "We are always happy to help."

"There's nothing that needs clarification," Beta Koin stated, the smile slipping from his features to be twisted into annoyance. "I'm here to pick up our rogue shifter. It's as simple as that." He pinned a narrow-eyed gaze on Miggs. "You should have known better than to hurt Kenny, Midget. If you had just fled, we may have let you go." Shaking his head, Beta Koin put an aggrieved expression on his face. "But instead, you went and harmed an innocent."

Miggs cringed as he pressed into Del's side.

"Relax, Miggs," Del rumbled. He kept his voice soothing even as he pinned a cold stare on Beta Koin. When Del spoke to the beta, his tone held that same coolness. "So, you're my father-in-law. Can't say I'm very impressed."

Beta Koin looked confused for a few seconds. Then he must have registered the way Del was holding Miggs and how his lover pressed against him. Disgust carved deep grooves into his face as he sneered at them.

Then Beta Koin cleared his expression and turned his attention back to the councilman. "It aggrieves me to learn that Midget coerced one of your men into mating with him before his crimes came to light." He shook his head, feigning sadness even as the room filled with the scent of his distaste. "As their mating must be new, I'm certain your enforcer will be just fine should we decide Midget must be put to death for his crimes."

"You speak so very callously of your own son." Councilman Colearian steepled his hands on the table, resting them on the folders. "Is that common in your muddle, Beta Koin?"

"Normally, no, Councilman," Beta Koin replied without missing a beat. "But as Midget is a murderer, I no longer consider him my son."

"I am not!" Miggs cried, clearly having had enough of his name being slandered. Pointing at his father, he declared, "I didn't kill anyone, and you know it. And don't worry. I haven't considered you a father in decades. Ever since you banished mom!"

Del snapped his focus to Miggs. "He did what?" he asked tightly.

Miggs nodded, nibbling his bottom lip.

As was becoming a habit, Del immediately reached up and tugged it free. "Tell me, my mate."

"There was a meeting, and then she never came back," Miggs told him. "Beta Koin said that she chose to leave, but he smelled of deceit. When I started questioning him, he" — Miggs paused and touched his cheek, wincing — "well, I didn't question things after that." Lowering his voice, he finished, "But I know Mom wouldn't have left on her own."

"We'll get to the bottom of that," Del assured Miggs. He would discover what happened to his mate's mother, since his speech radiated fondness and sadness for her in equal measure. Then Del focused on Beta Koin. "And Miggs and I are fated mates. As I am an enforcer for the Shifter Council, Miggs is now also under the council's protection and judgment. He won't be coming with you." Smirking at the beta, Del continued . . . just because he liked the angry expression beginning to darken the shifter's features. "Oh, and we know you're lying . . . about a great many things."

"That is preposterous," Beta Koin claimed, starting to rise from his seat. "Two men can't be fated mates."

"Sit down, Beta Koin," Councilman Colearian ordered, his tone holding a hard note.

The beta immediately obeyed.

"My own fated mate is a man . . . and human, so yes, Fate does sometimes pair those of the same sex," the councilman declared. "And we have some questions for you." Turning his attention to Enforcer Gierson, he stated, "Enforcer Gierson, if you would please escort Enforcer Omar to a waiting room. I would like to speak with Beta Koin alone, first."

"Of course, Councilman," Enforcer Gierson quickly stepped forward and grabbed Enforcer Omar's upper arm. "This way, Enforcer Omar."

"Just a minute, Councilman," Beta Koin cried, rising to his feet. "This is outrageous. I came on good faith, and now you're questioning me?"

Del curled his lip as he eased his hold on Miggs so he could take a step forward. "You came under false pretenses to kidnap and enslave my mate," he stated bluntly. "And I will not let that happen."

As Enforcer Gierson led an objecting Enforcer Omar from the room, Interrogator Malone stood and took up the enforcer's vacated position. He left the briefcase by his chair. Del urged Miggs to stay with Germaine and headed toward it.

As Del lifted it and placed it on the table, he eyed Beta Koin coldly. "Now then, Beta." He lifted a vial and a needle from the case. "Let's see if we can make you a little more cooperative. Hmm?"

Beta Koin's eyes widened, and he shook his head. Predictably, he lunged toward the door behind him, which was why Malone had moved. The beta's response had been expected.

Malone grabbed Beta Koin's arm, spun him around, and forced him back toward the table. Bending him at the waist, he pinned the man's face against the solid piece of oak. Then, with one hand at Koin's neck and the other holding one arm behind his back, Malone held him in place.

Del prepared a needle with the drug. It wouldn't harm the shifter and would wear off damn fast, considering their metabolisms. Still, with a potent enough dose, it would last long enough for Del to get the answers he needed.

Namely, what the hell really happened to Kenny, and why did the alpha name Miggs rogue?

# CHAPTER TEN

In the blink of an eye, Del transformed from Miggs's kind, thoughtful lover to a cold-hearted interrogator. He watched as his mate injected some pale-yellow fluid into Beta Koin's neck. Then he turned without a word and replaced the used items in the briefcase.

"Have him take a seat, Malone," Del ordered as he grabbed a chair for himself. While Malone obeyed, Del settled in his own seat. "We're going to ask you questions, Koin, and you're going to tell us the truth." Relaxing back, he placed his left ankle over his right knee and folded his hands behind his head. With a wide grin, Del claimed, "And if you don't, we're going to break something. We'll start with fingers, since those heal quickly and with little complications." Scoffing, Del stated, "Don't want you to have to take up too much of our healers' valuable time, now do we?"

"Y-You can't do th-this to m-me." Koin's voice came out a little slurred, and his stutters betrayed how he was struggling to control his words.

"Sure we can," Del replied, grinning. Except, no mirth or pleasure reached his hazel eyes. "After all, here we are."

Koin's eyes narrowed, and he turned his attention to Councilman Colearian. "When the r-rest of the council f-finds out about th-this—"

Councilman Colearian cut off the man's struggling words. "With the information I have on Alpha Shaun"—he tapped the folder on the table before him—"there will be no one to file grievances." The councilman looked beyond Koin to Del.

"Interrogator Delanrue, shall we begin?"

"With pleasure, Councilman." Del smirked coldly at Koin. "So, Koin, why did you and Alpha Shaun make Miggs a slave in the alpha's house?"

Even as Koin's features twisted in defiance, he replied, "He's a faggot. Good only for labor."

A muscle ticked in Del's jaw, betraying his anger at Koin's answer, even though Miggs knew it had to have been completely expected. "Are there any other members of your muddle being used as slave labor?"

Koin clenched his jaw, as if fighting against the urge to answer. Then he replied, "No. Now we trap them in their guinea pig form and sell them to pet stores."

Enforcer Dane growled low in his throat, clearly expressing his ire even better than the anger darkening his brown eyes nearly to black.

To Miggs's surprise, Koin actually laughed. His smile appeared a little drunken. "What?" With a smirk, he added, "Faggots are worthless to strengthening a muddle. At least this way, they can be put to some use."

"Who came up with the idea?" Del asked.

"Me," Koin replied, sounding proud.

Del finally lowered his arms and leaned forward, resting his left forearm on the table. He had his hand clenched in a fist, so tightly that his knuckles had turned white. His nostrils flared, but when he spoke again, his voice still held the same cutting chilliness.

"Where do you get the drugs?"

After a swallow so hard his Adam's apple bobbed, Koin ground out, "Alpha Shaun gets them."

"From whom?" Del pressed.

"I don't know," Koin responded.

Del and Malone exchanged a look that Miggs couldn't

hope to interpret. Malone moved swiftly from his position be-hind Koin. He grabbed the shifter's left wrist, gripped his pinky, and yanked.

Koin's scream filled the conference room.

Miggs cringed, wrapping his arms around his torso. When he felt a hand on his upper back, he nearly leaped out of his skin. Feeling the gentle touch rub up and down a little, Miggs turned and looked at Germaine, but the snake shifter wore an impassive expression and wasn't looking at him.

"We warned you," Del commented, looking at his nails with disinterest. "Wanna try again? Or should we break an-other finger?"

Miggs watched with bated breath as he took in his father's expression. He knew that look—the shifter wanted to deny knowledge again. His brown eyes burned with the hatred he felt as he stared at Del.

"Alpha Shaun gets it from some guy he calls Fox Nose," the beta finally said.

Malone lifted a hand and made a *so-so* gesture.

Del narrowed his eyes and leaned forward. "You know him by another name. What is it?"

Once more, Koin's jaw ticked.

Frowning, Miggs realized he'd heard that name before. *But where? Think!*

Miggs had worked at the alpha's home, behind the scenes, for years. He should have known what was happening, have seen something amiss. It wasn't just his own mother that had ended up disappearing.

*Fox Nose.*

Then it clicked. Just as Del arched one eyebrow, causing Malone to reach for Koin's wrist again, Miggs cried out, "Pro-fessor Gilly!"

All eyes turned to him, including his father's . . . which blazed with warnings of retribution if he didn't shut his mouth damn fast.

Feeling safe with Germaine at his side, Del in the room, and knowing the others would have his back, Miggs told them, "Professor Gilly is a science professor at the community college near our muddle. A number of us have gone there for some classes."

"Shut up," Koin hissed. "Y-You don't know what y-you're talking about."

Miggs ignored him, knowing if he'd been on the wrong track, his father wouldn't be bothered by him sharing the information. "He really is a fox shifter, and his nose resembles his animal while in human form. Even humans have taken to calling him Fox Nose." Cocking his head, Miggs searched his memory. "I . . . I think I saw him come to the alpha's house maybe . . . six times in the five years I worked there." Worked was a relative term, but it was easier to say it that way. "I always figured it was to pay tithe to continue living on the outskirts of our muddle lands, but considering how many different packs, prides, and such are in the area because the council is here . . ." Miggs trailed off with a wave of his hand.

"You've just signed your death warrant," Koin screamed, jumping from his seat. Then he lunged across the table, reaching for Miggs.

As Miggs jerked backward, slamming against the wall behind him, Germaine stepped forward, clearly ready to meet the challenge — not that Beta Koin would be much of a challenge to the much larger enforcer.

Del reached Koin first. Grabbing him from behind, he had the beta in a full nelson in the next instant. He snarled low in his throat, and anger burned in his hazel eyes, making them glow an almost golden color.

"Easy, Del," Dane rumbled, approaching slowly. "We still have a few questions. Remember?" His brother had his hands out in front of him, his palms out in placation. "You can't kill him, yet."

"He went after my fated mate." Del's voice came out low and angry, with a hissing quality that told everyone listening how close his dragon was to the surface. "That's a *death* sentence."

Miggs could see the desire, the *need* for retribution in Del's eyes. As much as he didn't want to see his mate kill his father, it wasn't for blood tie reasons. He agreed with Dane.

"Del," Miggs murmured, easing away from the wall. He stepped partially around Germaine, but the other shifter wouldn't let him get too close. "Del, look at me."

Slowly, Del's gaze panned right to focus on Miggs. He saw the anguish buried deep within their depths, the hint of fear. His mate had feared for his life, and that knowledge made Miggs's next words come easier.

"Del, my mate. I'm fine. Just fine." Miggs smiled reassuringly at his big shifter. "You stopped him, my love. You saved me. Ease your grip, so you can finish your job." Miggs saw Del's nostrils flare as his arms slowly loosened their tight hold. "That's the way. We need to know what they did with Kenny."

"And your mother," Del whispered.

Miggs nodded, although he feared she was long dead.

Before Del completely released his hold, he snarled into Koin's ear, "But since we can't have you thinking you can get away with that." Then he grabbed the beta's right arm in both hands and jerked.

The sound of bones snapping filled the room right before Koin screamed, "You bastard!" Since Del had let him go, the smaller shifter cradled his clearly broken arm to his chest. "I'll get you for this. I'll get you all—"

"Good grief," Malone cut in, clamping a hand on his shoulder. "You really don't get it, do you?" Using a foot, he turned around one of the chairs located on that side of the conference table. Then Malone shoved Koin into it before standing over him with his arms crossed. "You're a walking dead man, Koin. Your one decision is whether you're going to go out with dignity or not."

"I'm a muddle beta," Koin growled, although pain filled his voice. "You can't threaten me."

As soon as Del had released Miggs's father, he'd wrapped his arms around Miggs.

Miggs was only too happy to snuggle into his side. That didn't stop him from paying close attention to what was going on around him. Hearing his father's claim, Miggs scoffed and shook his head.

"You're so full of yourself that you can't accept what's happening to you even while it's happening," Miggs stated in wonder. "This is the Shifter Council. They don't mess around with the safety of our secret, and you and Alpha Shaun threatened it. How many others in the muddle are in on this plan?"

*Surely it couldn't just be those two.*

When Koin just glared back at Miggs, a hard sneer curving his lips, Malone stated, "Don't you worry, Miggs. We'll get that information out of him." He cracked his knuckles, adding, "I have aaaaaall afternoon." With a malicious smile that would have chilled Miggs to the bone had it been directed at him, Malone stared down at Koin. "You and me are gonna become really, *really* well acquainted."

"Since the serum wore off, are you going to give him another dose?" Dane asked curiously as he moved back to Councilman Colearian's side. "Because it'd be nice to know where to start looking for Kenny."

"A second dose so soon won't do much," Malone revealed as he pulled a cable out of his back pocket. "So we'll do this the hard way."

As Malone began to reach for Koin's hand — the one with the broken finger — Koin must have finally come to his senses. "No, wait." He tried to rear back in his seat, but he didn't really have anywhere to go. "I'll talk. No need for that."

Malone paused, slapping the cable against his thigh.

"What did you do with Kenny?" Del asked bluntly.

"Alpha Shaun sold him to a pet store," Koin replied quickly. "I don't know which one. I'm not part of that."

Miggs could hardly believe that. "Then what's your part it in?" he asked, unable to help his curiosity.

Curling his lip, Koin pinned a hate-filled stare at Miggs. "Keeping an eye on those in our muddle so the alpha can take care of our connections." Disgust once more coloring his features as he glanced between Del and Miggs, Koin added, "I let the alpha know about the degenerates and those useless to keeping our muddle strong."

"And my mom?" Miggs hated how tentative he sounded, but he couldn't help it. He'd wondered for so long, and now he would get his answer.

Del probably scented his unease, for he began rubbing his hand up and down Miggs's back, soothing him.

Koin began to shrug, but then he stopped and winced. "She met her fated mate, so she left the muddle."

Miggs felt his heart tighten in his chest.

*She really did leave? Without saying anything to me?*

Growling, Del rumbled, "Did you give her the opportunity to say goodbye?"

"She chose her mate over her duty," Koin stated with a sneer. "She was lucky we let her leave with the clothes on her back."

"Who is her mate?" Councilman Colearian asked, pen in hand. "Was he part of another muddle?"

Koin's face darkened, clearly displeased to have to be answering the question, but he did it. "Her mate was some woman named Glenda. I didn't ask for specifics." Sniffing derisively, Koin claimed, "I wasn't going to allow a degenerate anywhere near my child a moment longer." Then he scowled at Miggs. "So you being just as deviant didn't come as a surprise."

That also explained why Koin had kept such a close eye on him and why he'd urged Miggs to pick a girl and settle down, even though he was considered young in shifter terms.

"I think we've had enough of your asshole beta's presence," Del declared, tightening his hold on Miggs. "Do you need us any longer, Councilman Colearian?"

The councilman shook his head. "No, I think we have it covered. Thank you, Enforcer Delanrue." The aging grizzly shifter's smile turned kind as he focused on Miggs. "Now that we have testimony that you did not, in fact, kill Kenny, we will have all charges dropped in regards to you being rogue. Congratulations."

Relief flooded Miggs, and he nodded. "Thank you, Councilman."

After Councilman Colearian nodded and waved his hand, Del guided them out of the room.

Before the door closed, Miggs heard Koin holler, "Don't get comfortable here, Midget. Alpha Shaun will have his way!"

Miggs grimaced. Unable to help himself, he stopped and pressed his face against Del's chest. He held on tight to his mate and inhaled deeply. With Del's arms around him, returning the embrace, Miggs soaked up the soothing comfort of his lover.

"I should have saved you from that," Del murmured, nuzzling his cheek over Miggs's head. "I should have—"

"Stop," Miggs whispered, lifting his head. Bringing a hand around, he touched his fingertips to Del's lips, stopping him from voicing even more doubts. "I think I actually needed that," Miggs admitted, lowering his hand. "More than I realized. It gave me . . . closure."

"Did you want to track down your mother?" Del asked as he turned them and started walking them down the hall. "I bet she'd love to hear from you."

Miggs shrugged. "I'll think about it."

As Del nodded, he growled, "Damn it. I can't wait."

To Miggs's surprise, Del yanked open a door on the right and hurried them both inside. He found them in a closet full of cleaning supplies.

Even as Miggs opened his mouth to question Del, his lover grabbed the button on his jeans. "Seeing you in danger, even for a second," Del grumbled, shaking his head. "Never want to see that again." Revealing his huge, swollen rod, Del reached for Miggs's jeans next. "Have to have you. Have to assure myself you're okay. Safe with me."

Seeing the feral need in Del's eyes, coupled with the heavy scent of arousal that quickly flooded the small space, Miggs moaned. "Yessss!" he hissed, happy to shimmy out of his pants.

# CHAPTER ELEVEN

Del knew fucking in the hallway closet wasn't a good idea. That didn't mean he was going to stop. Miggs had been so close to being attacked . . . with him standing right there.

*I need to sink into him, to touch him, to stroke my hands over every inch of his body and verify that he's injury-free.*

His animal drove him hard to possess, to claim, to reassert their connection.

With Miggs's welcoming body—naked from the waist-down—pressed against him, Del yanked the single-use packet of lube from his pocket before shoving them down further. He lifted Miggs, pressing his back against the wall. To Del's pleasure, his mate immediately wrapped his legs around him.

Del kept one arm around Miggs's waist, holding him in place. Bringing the packet to his mouth, he tore it open with his teeth. He held it out to Miggs.

"Take this," Del ordered gruffly. "Pour it on my fingers."

Miggs immediately obeyed, taking it. "Have you always carried these?" he asked as he poured the slick onto Del's fingers.

Hearing the note of jealousy in Miggs's word, Del grinned. "Only since I met you," he told him, moving his hand beneath Miggs's bottom. As he pushed one finger deep into his mate's hot channel, Del winked and told him, "Was recommended by another enforcer who recently mated."

Instead of answering, Miggs tipped his head back, resting it on the wall, and moaned.

Del grinned, satisfaction flooding him upon the knowledge that he'd found Miggs's prostate on the first try. He eased his finger out, then pushed it back in again. Since his mate was partially stretched from their early morning bout, one finger quickly became two, then three.

Seeing Miggs rock in his hold, clearly enjoying Del's ministrations, along with the way his face had flushed and his cock jutted from his groin, drove Del's own need even higher. His dick throbbed and twitched. He felt a bead of pre-cum slide across his crown, sending tingles to his balls.

Unable to wait a second longer, Del eased his fingers from Miggs's clenching channel.

Miggs whimpered, his fingers digging into Del's shoulders. "Hurry."

"I am," Del assured, gripping his shaft. He gritted his teeth upon feeling the stimulus to his hard flesh. After a couple of swipes to coat himself with the remaining slick, Del guided his crown to Miggs's prepared hole. "Push out."

Del didn't wait for a response. He couldn't. With his need too great, he gave in to his animalistic base urge and thrust.

Miggs's body immediately gave way, and Del kept pushing, sinking deep into his mate's body, all the way to the root, in one long smooth glide.

Once Del had his balls pressed to Miggs's ass crack, he paused and let out a long groan. The pressure to his cock felt so damn exquisite. Every time he sank into his lover felt even better than the time before.

Del shifted his hold to each of Miggs's ass cheeks. Prying them apart a bit allowed him to sink just a smidge deeper into his forever love. The base of his spine already tingled, and his testicles threatened to draw up.

Unwilling to lose it so quickly, Del focused on Miggs's features. He took in his mate's glazed expression and slightly parted lips. His lover rested his head against the wall and peered up at him through heavy-lidded eyes.

"Del," Miggs whispered, pleasure and need making his voice rough. "S-So good. You always feel so good."

"So do you," Del replied just as gruffly. Dipping his head, he rested his forehead against the wall beside Miggs's, placing his mouth close to his mate's ear. "You called me your love."

Miggs turned his head a little and nuzzled their temples together. "Yeah. Hope that's okay."

"More than," Del confirmed. Then he admitted, "Loved you damn near from the second I met you."

"I was a mess," Miggs whispered back, sounding confused. "Couldn't even make one decision."

Del turned his head so he could lick at Miggs's temple, relishing the taste of his mate. "That's what I'm here for. To help with anything you need, my little love."

Miggs nodded, then turned his head and met his gaze. "Love you, too." Before Del could reply, Miggs urged, "And now I need you to move."

Then Miggs clenched his chute muscles, squeezing Del's erection in an exquisite vise. He relaxed before doing it again.

Groaning, Del held still, reveling in the way the sensation went damn near straight to his balls.

"Move," Miggs urged, nipping at his ear. "Massage my prostate. Give your mate what he needs."

Unable to deny any request from his little mate, Del obeyed. He lifted his head a bit and peered between them. Easing his hips backward, he watched his erection appear from Miggs's gorgeous hole.

Del paused for an instant when his crown stretched Miggs's ring. His cock throbbed, attempting to twitch, but was held securely in position by his swollen head still in his mate's body. Moaning at the sensations, Del slowly sank back into his mate, watching himself take his man.

Miggs moaned into his ear, and the sound was music to Del's ears. The hairs on his arms stood on end, and his control began to slip. He only managed to watch himself take his mate twice more because the visual was just too much to resist before his need became too great.

Releasing Miggs's ass cheek with his right hand, Del wrapped that arm tight around his lover's waist. He moved his left forearm to the wall beside his mate's head. Holding Miggs steady, Del began a steady pounding.

Sweat dripped from Del's temples as he sawed into Miggs's hole over and over. The skin of his rod sliding within the depths of his mate sent delicious zings to his balls, which spread out through his groin. When the base of his spine began to tingle, he somehow managed to speed up his ruts.

"Del!"

Miggs's breathy cry, the sweet scent of his mate's release perfuming the air, and the feel of his lover's chute clenching upon him all combined to yank Del over the edge and into bliss.

Letting out a rough cry of his own, Del held his lover steady as he poured his release into him. Each burst of his balls sent a wave of ecstasy coursing through him. His body shuddered with aftershocks, and Del had to lock his knees to keep them from falling.

When Miggs began mouthing kisses along Del's neck, he hummed and tilted his head, offering his lover more room. He loved his mate's mouth on him, and he would take it any way he could get it. Even the scrape of his teeth over his flesh didn't pull Del from his post-coital haze.

The stab of teeth into the flesh where his neck met his shoulder yanked Del back to the here and now. Then tingles flooded his chest, and his nipples beaded pleasantly. The sensation shot straight to his balls, and to Del's shock, a fresh orgasm blind-sided him.

As Del bucked his hips once, then buried his length deep into Miggs once more, he groaned as he rode out the heady sensation. Spots danced across his vision as his balls unloaded over and over. His dick continued to throb, as if Miggs were sucking on his prick instead of his neck.

Finally, Miggs eased his teeth free, and Del managed to suck in a much-needed breath. With his legs feeling like jelly, he turned them. Del allowed his feet to slide from under him, and he eased down the wall.

Del landed on his ass with a soft thump and let out a long sigh of satiation. "Damn, Miggs," he mumbled, easing his hand under his mate's shirt so he could rub over his back. "So that's how that feels."

Miggs rested his temple just below Del's shoulder and peered at him through his lashes. "Hope you didn't mind. I couldn't help myself." His brows furrowed as Miggs admitted, "You got into a fight for me, and I . . . I guess—"

When Miggs stopped talking, clearly struggling, Del smiled. He threaded his fingers through his shifter's hair and finished for him, "You needed the connection."

Miggs nodded.

Dipping his head, Del pressed a light kiss to Miggs's lips before he told him, "I loved every second of it, and you are welcome to bite me anytime."

The way Miggs beamed at him told Del that he'd said the right thing.

Del felt his dick begin to soften, and he realized that it was time to move the party to their own room.

"Come on, my sweet." Del encouraged Miggs to get his feet under him. "Let's get dressed and back to our room." Smiling wryly, he added, "We'll see if we can get there without too much razzing."

Ten minutes later, Del spotted Dakota coming from the opposite direction.

His brother appeared concerned at first and began by saying, "Hey, Dane texted me. Told me what happened. I didn't find you in your room and wondered — " By then, Dakota had drawn close enough to get a whiff of their scent. Barking a laugh, he grinned broadly. "Oooohhh, so that's what took you so long."

"Shut up, asshole," Del snapped, but he couldn't help but grin, too.

Dakota reached over and tugged his shirt away from his shoulder. Even as Del pulled away from him, his brother beamed at him. "Hot damn, man. Congrats." Then he held out a fist before Miggs. "Nice mark, Miggs."

Even though Miggs's face had turned bright red, he gamely returned Dakota's fist-bump, saying, "Thanks."

"Are you sure you're okay with me going back to work?" Del asked from where he sat on the end of the bed. "They still haven't tracked down your ex-alpha."

Del hated the fact that Shaun and a couple of the enforcers that had ended up involved had somehow managed to give their trackers the slip. Maybe it was because Koin hadn't checked in in a reasonable timeframe, but the alpha's home had been abandoned. Not only that, but his computers had been wiped, and the laptops and hard drives were gone.

*He'd had an escape plan in place. So where would he go?*

Fortunately, they'd managed to scoop up Professor Gilly. The number of people *that* shifter had been able to implicate was . . . daunting. That was one of the reasons Head Enforcer Mycroft had asked Del to return to duty after only a week-and-a-half off with his mate.

They were seriously understaffed for all the problems they were rooting out.

"It's fine, Del," Miggs assured, smiling so sweetly from his place sitting against the headboard. He held up his tablet and said, "I'm researching recipes for pastries, and I'm going to meet up with Desmond in the kitchens. He said he'd help me make one of them."

Del nodded, knowing Desmond was a red fox shifter who worked in the massive kitchens for the council's headquarters. He was a nice guy, who didn't mind speaking out against problems, regardless of the source. The guy also cooked a mean steak with all the delicious sides.

"You're doing that today?" Del asked, rising so he could finish buttoning his shirt. "I totally forgot."

Of course, that could have been caused by the brain-melting sex they'd enjoyed that morning. As Del recalled the taste of Miggs's cum on his tongue, he swept his gaze over his naked mate's torso. Narrowing his eyes, he wondered if he had time for a quickie.

Miggs snickered. Grabbing a pillow, he used it to cover his chest. "No," he stated, pointing at him. "You go to work. I want to soak in the tub while I look at recipes before I have to go to the kitchen, and I need to be able to walk at least semi-normal in public."

Groaning, Del adjusted his semi-plump dick before striding toward his lover. "Okay," he grumbled good-naturedly. Leaning down, Del pressed a light kiss to his mate's delectable lips. "I'll seek you out in the kitchen for lunch."

After getting a confirmation from Miggs, Del pecked his mate's lips again. Then he turned and hurried from the room while he still could. When others had talked about mates, no one had ever told him about how difficult it was to leave them and go to their job every day.

Shaking his head at himself, Del locked the door behind him and strode down the hallway. He and Miggs had decided to stay there for the time being . . . at least until the rogues from his mate's muddle were caught. There had been no way

Del would have felt comfortable taking his mate to live in his home—regardless that it was near to his brothers' places.

Dane and Dakota had completely understood. The pair had even half-moved into their suites at the complex, too. When Del had told his brothers that it wasn't necessary, they'd scowled at him and reminded him how family always came first.

Del had thanked them and dropped the subject.

Reaching Councilman Lorian Bakerman's office, Del knocked. The door was immediately opened to reveal Enforcer Igor. The massive gray wolf shifter stepped backward and beckoned him into the office.

"Ah, welcome, Enforcer Delanrue," Councilman Bakerman greeted from behind his desk. A wry smile curved the man's full lips. "I heard you're with us today. Thank you for being so flexible."

While Del couldn't remember the last time he'd acted as a bodyguard for a councilman, he knew their ranks were spread too thin, and everyone had to pitch in. After all, he didn't have anyone to interrogate at the moment. While Del had been on vacation settling his bond with his mate, Malone and two other interrogators had cleared out their cells.

*Hopefully, we'll fill them with Shaun and his people soon.*

"It's my honor to assist the council in any way that I can," Del told the buffalo shifter, moving closer to the desk. "May I ask how many meetings we're sitting through today?"

"Sadly, three," the councilman replied with a grimace. "One with a vampire council representative. Another with a pack alpha from Florida." He tapped at his tablet's surface and winced. "Damn."

Del cocked his head. "Something wrong?"

"The third's an early brunch with my mother."

From the pained way Councilman Bakerman admitted that, Del couldn't help but ask, "Is that a problem?"

The councilman sighed deeply, his shoulders sagging.

"No, it just means I'm going to be fielding all kinds of set-up attempts . . . again."

Fighting back a chuckle, Del struggled to keep a straight face.

Almost three hours later, as Del listened to Councilman Bakerman's mother ask for the third time why he hadn't found a nice girl to settle down with, Del appreciated that he'd never experienced having a mother meddle in his love life.

When an alert chimed through his phone, Del almost felt grateful for the interruption . . . until he checked in for an update and learned the disturbance was in the cafeteria.

*My mate is supposed to be in those kitchens right now.*

# CHAPTER TWELVE

After a relaxing bath, which soothed not only his nerves at going out alone that day as well as his slightly tender hole, Miggs prepared to head to the cafeteria. He would never ask his well-endowed lover to control his enthusiasm for his body, and in truth, he loved the after-effect. He just didn't want to waddle down the hallway.

Plus, the bath really had given Miggs the perfect amount of time to find a couple of pastry recipes to show Desmond. He'd met the fox shifter while in the cafeteria a few days before when he'd been pouring over the buffet's cookie choices. When Miggs had explained he was trying to decide on a couple for Del, Desmond had been able to give him some pointers.

Evidently, Desmond had worked as one of the cooks for almost seventeen years. He was familiar with just about everyone's food preferences. Desmond had even revealed that Del had a sweet tooth.

Normally, Del did all the cooking. When Miggs had asked about that once, his mate had explained about his driving instinct to provide for him. Since Miggs had always loved dabbling in the kitchen, he couldn't wait to do something in return for his mate, making him a yummy treat since Del had no baking abilities.

*Something I can do for him.*

Miggs grabbed his tablet and his keys. After sliding his feet into a pair of shoes, he opened the door. He locked up and headed toward the cafeteria.

Using the back hallway Desmond had told him about, Miggs bypassed the cafeteria and reached the kitchen. He peeked inside and swept his gaze around the area. While several people bustled around the space and dishes clacked in the sink by those washing them, the room didn't seem too busy.

"Hey, man," a dark-haired man called, spotting him. "You lost?"

"Um, I'm looking for Desmond," Miggs told him, doing his best not to sound timid.

"Oh, are you Miggs?" the guy asked, crossing to him.

Miggs nodded. "Yeah. That's me."

The man held out his hand. "I'm Bart. Come on in." He beckoned him inside. "Desmond said he was expecting you. He went to deliver some food to the buffet, but he should be back in a sec." Bart guided Miggs toward a back section of the kitchen. "He set up some stuff back here. Said something about a baking lesson?"

Nodding again, Miggs peered around the industrial space. "Yeah. Said he could help me make something for my mate. He has a sweet tooth."

Bart grinned. "Nice. Who's your mate?"

"Enforcer Delanrue Drudeson." Miggs couldn't keep the pride out of his voice or the grin off his face. He loved being bonded with the sexy shifter.

With wide eyes, Bart murmured, "You bagged *that* Drudeson brother? Oh, damn!" Just as quickly, he smirked. "He's the intense one. Bet that translates to some fantastic moments in the sack." With a shoulder roll, Bart added, "Unless he's a selfish asshole."

Miggs growled softly. "Watch it, Bart," he warned, surprised at his sudden urge to smack the guy upside the head. "My mate's amazing . . . in and out of bed, not that it's any of your business."

"Sorry, Miggs," Desmond cut into the conversation. "Ignore Bart's mouth. He has no filter and often doesn't know when to keep his mouth shut."

Bart looked truly confused. "What'd I say?"

Desmond's expression turned pained. "See what I mean?" Then he turned back to Bart. "I got it here. Thanks for showing Miggs in."

Nodding, still appearing as if he didn't get why he'd just been yelled at, the dark-haired shifter headed back to work.

"Really. Sorry about Bart," Desmond repeated with a wry smile. "He doesn't mean anything by it."

Miggs understood that and nodded. "It's fine." Chuckling self-consciously, he admitted, "Never felt that kind of possessive jealousy before. It was weird."

Humming, Desmond reminded him, "You're newly mated. I'm sure it'll tone down after a decade or two." With a wink, he added, "Or so I've been told." Before Miggs could figure out how to respond to that, Desmond held out his hand. "Okay, so let's see what you've picked out."

Turning on his tablet, Miggs pulled up what he'd chosen and handed it to the cook.

Over half an hour later, Miggs washed flour and dough from his hands, scrubbing under his fingernails. He dried his hands, then stared at the oven. He hoped the strawberry cupcakes turned out.

"Ready to start making the icing?" Desmond asked, leaning a hip on the counter beside him. "It'll have time to set in the fridge while that first batch cools and the second batch cooks. It'll be perfect."

"As long as it doesn't take me three times as long to make as the recipe says like it did the cupcakes," Miggs said dryly. "Fifteen minutes, my ass."

Desmond barked a laugh. "I'm sure it won't. In fact, the

shortcut I'm going to show you will guarantee that —"

A loud crash drew both their attentions. A second later, more breaking glass reached their ears, and Miggs realized it came from the cafeteria proper beyond the swinging doors.

"Bummer," Desmond murmured with a grimace. "Sounds like one of the busboys is having an off day."

Unable to help himself, Miggs eased to one of the large openings that allowed the cooks to look out at the buffet so they could monitor the food. He swept his gaze over the area, quickly spotting the disturbance. Several people were throwing dirty looks at a pair of big men who were ordering everyone to leave.

The sandy-blond-haired bruiser seemed to be in charge, with a dark-haired, equally large guy doing his bidding. Except, they weren't the ones who caused Miggs's blood to freeze in his veins. A whimper escaped him, and he jerked back from the window. He struggled to catch his breath as he pressed his palm to his chest.

*How could he be here?*

"What the hell is Enforcer Glade doing?" Desmond grumbled, shaking his head. Then he must have noticed Miggs's distress, for he gripped his shoulders and squeezed. "Miggs? What's wrong?" When Miggs couldn't manage to answer right away, Desmond asked, "Are you reacting to an allergy?"

"N-No, I—" Knowing he had to get himself together, he swallowed hard, then met Desmond's gaze. "One of the men out there is my ex-alpha, Shaun. He's supposed to be a wanted shifter. How could he get in here?"

"You're sure?" Desmond asked. As soon as Miggs nodded, the fox shifter hurried over to the intercom and pressed a button. "Red alert in the cafeteria and the kitchens."

"Mycroft is already on his way," a female voice replied. "You should see him shortly. More are en route."

The back door opened, and the redhead Miggs remembered from his first day out of the cell rushed into the kitchen.

"He's here," Desmond stated into the box. Then he turned to the redhead and dipped his head respectfully. "Enforcer Mycroft, since you got here so fast, I assume you know what's going on?"

"Yep," Mycroft replied with a growl in his voice. "An asshole helping another asshole." He pinned his green-eyed gaze on Miggs. "I want you to shift and hole up. Got it?"

Miggs nodded, then immediately began yanking off his clothes.

Mycroft focused back on Desmond. "You got any good hidey-holes in here, Des?" He glanced around the space. "Somewhere a small shifter could hide that would mask their scent?"

Desmond cocked his head for a second, then nodded. "Yeah, depending on size."

"Show Miggs," Mycroft ordered even as he toed off his sneakers and whipped his shirt over his head. "Feel free to shift, but stay out of the way of the big guns until reinforcements arrive. Huh?"

Even though he looked a little pale, Desmond scoffed. "Not shifting against animals like Glade and Theron." He grabbed a massive butcher knife from the block.

Miggs lost track of the conversation as he shifted. His body shrank as his bones popped, his tendons snapped, and his muscles cracked. He opened his eyes, and the world seemed massive around him.

"Damn, Miggs," Desmond murmured from where he crouched to his left. "You're a cute little thing." Holding out his hand, he told him, "If you step on, I'm going to hide you in the spice rack."

Miggs hesitated only an instant, then decided he could trust his new friend. Scurrying forward, he climbed onto the man's hand. He left his back legs on Desmond's palm and gripped his shirt cuff with his front ones.

"Okay," Desmond muttered, lifting him high into the air. "Be careful up here, okay?" He settled his hand on the edge of a shelf full of spices. After moving a couple aside with his free hand, Desmond ordered, "Slip behind them, and don't make any noise."

Obeying, Miggs carefully crawled off Desmond's hand, doing his best not to scratch the other shifter. He eased between the spice jars. His senses were immediately assaulted by a myriad of aromas, and he understood exactly why he'd been put there. The hiding place was even better than behind garbage cans.

Plus, so few people looked up when searching for something . . . or someone.

Miggs heard the clinking of glass and glanced behind him, seeing Desmond closing the gap behind him. Then his new friend headed to the stove, which was buzzing. He grabbed a hot pad, opened the oven, and pulled out the tray of cupcakes.

Even as Miggs wished he could smell them, he spotted the swinging door opening. Half a dozen men trooped into the kitchen. The dirty-blond guy was in the lead, followed by ex-alpha Shaun.

Four others followed. While Miggs knew one was an enforcer from his muddle, he didn't know the others.

"Enforcer Glade, why are you leading a rogue around shifter headquarters?" Mycroft asked, his tone mild as he addressed the dirty-blond-haired guy. Without waiting for an answer, Mycroft pinned a hard glare at the huge dark-haired man. "And Enforcer Theron, you are definitely the last person I would have thought would be helping rogues, seeing as your parents were slaughtered by them."

Enforcer Theron frowned. "Rogues?" He glanced around the group before landing his dark gaze on Enforcer Glade. "Enforcer Glade, what's going on?"

"Aaaahhh, he didn't tell you." Mycroft shook his head.

"Step away from them, Theron. You don't want to get involved in this mess."

Theron seemed to be wavering, glancing around the group uncertainly.

Enforcer Glade growled under his breath and pointed at Theron. "Don't do it," he ordered the other man. "I don't know what that little rogue has on Mycroft to make him defend him, but this is not our head enforcer speaking right now."

Mycroft smirked as he shook his head. Instead of addressing Glade, who seemed like a big douche who didn't want to listen to anyone but himself, he addressed Miggs's ex-alpha. "Shaun Rudger, I'm putting you and your ex-enforcer, Kitner Weiss, under arrest for a multitude of crimes, including drugging members of your muddle, shifter trafficking, and jeopardizing the secrecy of paranormals."

As Mycroft spoke, Theron's bronzed complexion paled. "Shit," the huge shifter muttered with wide eyes. Pointing at the guinea pig ex-alpha, he asked, "He really do all that?"

"Of course, he didn't," Glade countered, scowling. "That's bullshit that the rogue Midget Suvergy is trying to pin on him to get away with his own crimes."

"There is testimony of his crimes by others —" Mycroft began, but was cut off by a belligerent Glade.

"Yeah, by his own father." Glade scoffed. "His father! No wonder he's trying to help clear him. He's —"

"Enough," Shaun roared, clearly tired of the debate. "Where is he? I want him!"

"You'll find nothing here but your death," Mycroft warned. His eyes narrowed, and he pinned a hard gaze on Glade. "And that goes for anyone here who continues to back him."

"He was vetted by Councilman Peregrine," Glade claimed

with a sneer. "His word is above reproach. Far more trustworthy than you."

The creak of metal bending filled the air followed by the crunch of tile breaking. A low hissing roaring noise filled the area, followed by the thud of a table hitting a wall.

Mycroft shook his head, a smirk curving his lips. "Too late. Miggs's mate isn't going to let anything happen to him."

In the next instant, a massive lizard-like head appeared in the open window. A forked tongue flicked out, scenting the occupants of the room. The komodo dragon's attention swung to Shaun, perhaps because he was obviously a guinea pig shifter.

"Oh, fuck," Theron whispered. With wide eyes, he looked at Glade. "You went after Delanrue's new mate? And you dragged me into it? What the hell, man?" Lifting his hands, Theron began maneuvering away from the group and easing toward Mycroft. "I'm so sorry, Enforcer Delanrue. I'll make restitution. I didn't realize I was escorting a rogue or that these guys were after your mate."

Del flicked out his tongue toward Theron, obviously scenting him. Then he dismissed him and focused on the five still standing together. He hissed again, the sound full of anger and malice.

"I'm not letting this asshole stop me from my duties," Glade declared, tearing his shirt from his body. "I'll distract Delanrue. You guys take out these guys, find the rogue, and get the hell out of here. The councilman will get this sorted later."

A second later, Glade shifted and lunged out the swinging door. Del's dragon head pulled back out of sight. The sounds of outraged hisses, growling snarls, and bodies destroying furniture filtered through the air.

Miggs didn't have time to wonder about them for long. The kitchen erupted into pandemonium. Everyone shifted . . .

even Desmond.

Mycroft's cheetah worked in tandem with Theron's Kodiak bear, taking on a pair of strangers who turned into a couple of big tigers. Desmond's red fox raced around the kitchen, snapping and lunging at the pair of guinea pigs while deftly escaping the tigers' claws. The pair of guinea pigs seemed to be doing their best to distract Mycroft and Theron so that the tigers could get in a lucky shot.

Hunching against the back wall, Miggs could do nothing but watch and wait.

Fortunately, he didn't have to wait long.

An especially loud crash followed by a clearly feline yowl erupted in the air. A second later, Del's head returned, and it wasn't the only one. A pair of almost as large komodo dragon heads flanked him on each side.

The dragon on the right climbed along that wall while the one on the left did the same on the other. The pair each snapped up a tiger and dragged them through the huge opening, disappearing into the cafeteria.

Desmond seemed to have used the distraction to his advantage, for once they were gone, he yipped happily. His front paws stood on an overturned pot. He sniffed at the pot, then pranced on his back end as his tongue lolled.

Mycroft shifted in seconds, then glanced around the room. Pinning a gaze on Miggs, he smiled. He nodded, then moved toward Desmond.

"You get one or both under there?" Mycroft asked with a grin.

Yipping twice, Desmond looked clearly pleased with himself.

Chuckling, Mycroft nodded. "Good job." Then he turned to he focused on Del. "Is Glade alive out there?"

Del's eyes narrowed as the creature grumbled. Then the dragon nodded once.

Mycroft hummed, shaking his head. "I can only imagine how much restraint that took. Thank you." He headed to the spice rack and moved aside a couple of vials, revealing Miggs. "Your mate is safe and sound."

When Mycroft began reaching for Miggs, Del hissed. Lifting his hands in placation, the head enforcer backed away.

Crawling halfway through the window, crushing a prep island in the process, Del stretched out his neck and placed his head beside the shelf. He hiss-crooned softly.

Miggs crept forward, chittering. Since his mate wasn't changing back, he wasn't certain what he should do. If he shifted on the shelf, he would fall off . . . which would hurt.

"Crawl onto Del's head, Miggs," Mycroft encouraged. "He needs to stay in his dragon form until he has you somewhere safe." The cheetah shifter shrugged. "You haven't been together long, and you've been in too much danger. Just go with it."

Nodding, Miggs carefully climbed onto Del's broad flat head. As soon as he did so, his mate began withdrawing from the room. He barely had time to notice the destruction of the cafeteria furniture and dents in the walls before Del was hustling from the room.

"I'll give you an update tomorrow," Mycroft called, laughing.

Del hissed but didn't stop moving.

As they rushed through the hallways, heading for their suite, Miggs decided he didn't have a problem with his dragon's over-protective nature.

*Especially since I know exactly what will happen when we get to our room.*

Anticipation thrummed through Miggs as he looked forward to Del's special brand of making certain he didn't have any injuries.

*Hell yeah!*

They would figure everything else out later.

With a guinea pig grin, as Miggs was carried off by his dragon as if he were a damsel in distress, he thought of a line from one of his favorite movies.

*Tomorrow is another day.*

*And with my ex-alpha caught, now I'll have plenty of tomorrows to look forward to.*

Miggs couldn't have been happier.

YOU MAY ALSO ENJOY THE FOLLOWING
FROM EXTASY BOOKS INC:

*Luring the Polar Bear*
Charlie Richards

Excerpt

As Dixon crossed the room, a scent other than the food teased his nostrils. The pleasing aroma caused his blood to heat, and an unexpected bloom of arousal made his gut clench. He inhaled, but by the next step, the smell was gone.

Shaking his head, Dixon frowned and continued on. He stopped at the end of the buffet and picked up a tray. After placing a plate and roll of silverware on it, Dixon started toward the food.

Except, that same smell distracted him—strong, thick, and clearly masculine.

Dixon's mouth watered for a whole new reason. His dick plumped behind the fly of his jeans. His heart rate sped up.

Freezing, Dixon tipped his head back and took a deep breath. He barely managed to swallow his moan. The delicious aroma was close.

"You all right?" Manon asked softly, a look of concern on his face.

Am I? What's going on with me?

Then realization hit him like a two-by-four upside the head.

Meeting Manon's gaze, Dixon muttered in shock, "I think I scent my mate."

Manon's dark eyes widened but only for an instant. Then a wide smile curved his lips. He glanced around as if he would be able to tell who it was.

"That's great, Beta Dixon," Manon stated, returning his focus to him. "I think everyone in here is a shifter. Should make claiming him or her easy, right?"

Dixon snorted, shaking his head. "You really think so? Finding my mate here?" He set his tray down, no longer interested in food. "The prevalent opinion until recently was that Fate didn't make homosexual pairings, and the scent is definitely masculine. Thank the gods."

"Want me to whip you up a tray while you track down the source?" Manon offered. "Maybe you can have a meal with the guy and get to know him."

"Thanks, Manon," Dixon murmured distractedly, surveying the area. "I appreciate it."

Manon patted him on the shoulder. "Good luck."

Nodding absently, Dixon moved away from the buffet. He wandered slowly around the room, changing direction when the fantastic smell grew fainter. Tracking the scent in the large, air-conditioned cafeteria ended up more difficult than Dixon had thought it would be.

Or my mate's scent is all over the room.

When Dixon walked past a big blond man bussing a table, he finally received his first lungful of the scent directly from the source. His cock went ramrod straight behind his fly. He even felt his nipples bead.

Oh, hot damn, that's good.

Taking in the way the shifter placed the dishes someone had left on the table into a large blue tub, Dixon understood how the scent had ended up everywhere. His mate worked in the cafeteria. With his mate distracted, he took a few seconds to admire the man Fate had deemed the other half of his soul.

The stranger had broad shoulders, a thick neck, and heavily muscled limbs. His biceps stretched the short sleeves of his polo shirt enticingly, and his rather ragged-looking jeans caressed his meaty ass deliciously. Even the obvious pooch and love handles couldn't detract from the man's gorgeous physique.

Dixon wanted to explore every inch of the big shifter's six-foot-four-inch body. With the man topping him by an inch, he figured it would be an adjustment to kiss someone taller than himself, but he would be happy to make it. The plump lips on the man's boy-next-door features begged to be sucked and nibbled.

Finally, the shifter inhaled deeply, and his attention snapped to Dixon. His hazel eyes were wide in his tanned face, and confusion filled them. He furrowed strawberry-blond brows that matched the ear-length tresses on his head.

"Hello, mate," Dixon greeted, figuring it was best to start as he meant to go—straightforward and honest. "Will you tell me your name?"

"Mate?"

The man's deep voice wrapped around Dixon's senses, causing his dick to twitch.

Then the guy shook his head, his hazel eyes twinkling. "Naw. I ain't your mate." Even as he denied their connection, he grinned. "Fate don't pair two dudes. My brother explained it to me." He nodded as if what he was saying was completely accurate. "He told me even though I occasionally think a guy is hot, I can't act on it, because then Fate will never bring me my real mate."

"Your brother told you this?" Dixon asked instead of immediately claiming his brother was wrong. That wouldn't win him any points. "When?"

Shrugging massive shoulders, the shifter told him, "Any time he catches me lookin' at a guy." His face took on a pinkish hue as he reached down and adjusted the clearly defined erection behind his fly. "He's real smart. Not like me." He broke eye contact and returned to filling his tub. "So, even though you smell real good and my dick is drippin', I can't touch. Then I'll never get a real mate. Sorry."

Dixon's mind reeled as he processed everything the man had rambled. He clearly believed everything his brother had told him to the point of not acknowledging their connection. Before Dixon could come up with a viable counter, the man glanced his way and spoke again.

"Um, anyway. I gotta get back to work."

Then he hustled toward the kitchen.

"Not go as planned?"

Dixon jerked his gaze from the closed door. He'd been staring at it long enough that the swinging door had stopped moving. His focus pinned on Manon.

"Afraid not," Dixon replied softly. "Told you it wouldn't." Seeing the second tray Manon held, he turned and tipped his chin toward the table with the others, noticing how they were staring. "Seems I need to ask a few questions about my mate."

My mate, sadly, seemed a bit . . . dim.

That would make it easy for a dominating brother to manipulate.

When they reached the table, Dixon didn't even have to ask.

Vincentius sniffed the air, obviously catching the smell of his arousal. "If you were coming onto Helsinki, it probably won't work." The lion shifter's expression pinched. "He's on probation after being caught with the rogues, working as a guard." Grimacing, Vincentius added, "The only reason he isn't in the dungeons awaiting punishment is because Helsinki was doing as his brother, Rian, instructed him."

"Did Rian get into trouble?" Dixon asked curiously.

If Helsinki is already away from Rian's influence, that would help me.

"Sadly, no," Vincentius revealed with a grimace. "Rian is a

bouncer at a club, and he claims to have heard about a security opening on a councilman's staff and thought of his brother." Holding Dixon's gaze, he shrugged. "Rian wasn't aware of which councilman, but he told his brother about the position anyway and gave Helsinki the contact information to a guy who happened to be a rogue."

"So Helsinki didn't know," Dixon mused softly as he picked up a fried chicken strip. Manon knew him well. As Dixon dipped the end into a tub of honey mustard, he held Vincentius's gaze. "Well, I'm going to need to know everything about Helsinki. He's my mate."

Vincentius's eyes widened. "Well, fuck."

Before popping the meat into his mouth, Dixon winked. "Yeah. I hope to do that soon."

Dixon's still-hard dick twitched at the thought, his body more than on board with that idea.

# About the Author

Charlie started writing fantasy when she was eight, and after stumbling onto her first erotic romance at age nineteen, she realized her true calling. She now focuses on writing gay erotic romance, normally of the paranormal variety, with heroes of all kinds. With the help and support of her husband, Charlie finally fulfilled one of her life-long goals . . . move to acreage with her horses. You can often find her curled up with her laptop and a cup of tea or glass of wine, creating her next adventure. Charlie enjoys exploring the mountains of her new Oregon home on horseback, 4-wheeler, or motorcycle.

She can be reached at ch.richards2010@yahoo.com
Or visit her at www.charlie-richards.com

www.ingramcontent.com/pod-product-compliance
Lightning Source LLC
Chambersburg PA
CBHW070756120626
46557CB00002B/617